WALL STREET JOURNAL & USA TODAY
BESTSELLING AUTHOR

KB WINTERS

Copyright and Disclaimer

This book is a work of fiction. The names, characters, places and incidents are products of the writer's imagination and have been used fictitiously and are not to be construed as real. Any resemblance to persons, living or dead, actual events, locales or organizations is entirely coincidental.

Copyright © 2017 BookBoyfriends Publishing

All rights reserved. No part of this publication may be reproduced, stored in or introduced into a retrieval system, or transmitted, in any form, or by any means (electronic, mechanical, photocopying, recording, or otherwise) without the prior written permission of the copyright owner. The author acknowledges the trademarked status and trademark owners of various products referenced in this work of fiction, which have been used without permission. The publication/use of the trademarks is not authorized, associated with, or sponsored by the trademark owners.

CASH

CAOS MC BOOK TWO

By KB WINTERS

CASH

Prologue

***Minx** ~ Two months earlier*

I left Talon and Mick happily canoodling in front of all of Brently at their engagement party. Talon was the nicest woman I'd ever met, and no one deserved this happiness more than she did. She'd come to Brently months ago to claim the inheritance from a father she thought died years ago and found love with a really great guy. A stand-up guy who'd never hit a woman or mistreat her. Who would make sure her happiness and safety was his top priority.

As happy as I was for her, I also felt a pang of longing for what she had. Not Mick, but the stability and love he represented. I wanted someone who'd look at me and see a beautiful woman who could be their forever. The problem was that my past made that difficult. I didn't want someone to look at me and see a project to fix. A problem to correct. And for some reason the one man who got my juices flowing, also seemed to have a hero complex. I'd only met one real hero in my life, and his own crew took him down.

Not that it mattered what kind of man I wanted or needed since all the guys in Brently and CAOS saw me as a little sister or a club mascot or some other condescending bullshit. All but one and he saw me as someone who needed to be saved. Fixed.

"Got one of those for me?"

I looked up from my cigarette into deep green eyes that always seemed to be smiling, kissable pink lips that urged a girl to forget his flaws. And my weakness, silky blond hair that hung just to his shoulders and usually, a leather strap kept it from covering up his gorgeous face. "You don't smoke." Because Cash "CJ" Johnson was a Boy Scout, a goody two-shoes who would never do something to ruin his All-American good looks or his G.I. Joe physique.

"I don't normally but I figured if I asked for one of your smokes you wouldn't run away from me." He leaned against the brick wall of Talon's diner, Black Betty, smiling at me as though I was the answer to his prayers. I wasn't the answer to anybody's fucking prayers.

"Can't take a little rejection, Cash?" I didn't know why I was always so bitchy to him, but I couldn't seem to help myself.

He shrugged but that piercing green gaze never left mine. "I can take it, but I don't think that's what you're doing. Is it?"

I wanted to say yes. To say something so hurtful and cutting that he'd leave me the hell alone for the rest of forever. But I wasn't a liar. "Why don't you tell me since you seem to know so much."

"I can't figure out if it's me specifically who rubs you the wrong way or any man who shows interest in you." His gaze trailed down my body heavily as if it was his hands, and I felt the telltale signs of desire lighting up all of my pleasure spots.

Handsome bastard. "I don't need to be fixed, Cash."

"I'm not trying to fix you, Minx. I think you're perfect even when you're prickly as hell." His lush mouth curved in a lazy grin that sent heat scrambling around my body. "I just want to know you."

"Fuck me, you mean," I jutted my hip to the side, full of sass, as my brow cocked into my hairline. That's always what men wanted. Hell, I'd been taken from a park and turned out because men wanted it so bad they were willing to pay for it, to break the law to have it.

He laughed and dammit the sound was deep and masculine, and it skated all over my body, making me want to purr. "I won't lie and say fucking you isn't on my list, but really I want to know more about you, Minx. Take you for dinner, maybe dancing or stargazing or some shit. Then we can get to all *that*. When you're ready."

Why did he have to make it sound so good? So nice? It was the one thing about him that I couldn't pretend to hate because it did it for me. In a big fucking way. "What if I said I'd go home with you tonight?"

"I'm a man, baby, I'll make you scream my name all night, and then I'll make you breakfast in the morning. But I'd still ask you to go out with me, get to know me, before deciding you hate me."

"I don't hate you."

"Good to know." He bit back a smirk. "So, about that date. Tomorrow night, I'll pick you up at seven."

I flicked away what was left of my cigarette and pushed off the wall. "How about tonight? Just tonight," I clarified.

"How about we start with tonight and see where it goes?"

"No thanks. Not interested." I turned to walk away, but he grabbed my arm and turned me back to face him.

"Yeah, I don't believe that shit for one second." Then his mouth crashed down onto mind, his tongue warm and soft and insistent against my lips, making it hard to breathe. Hard to remember that I should be pushing his presumptuous ass as far away as I could. Then his hands rested at my hips, and the sensation did something to me I couldn't explain. When I gasped, his tongue swept between my lips and explored the depths of my mouth in a way I hadn't thought possible. The kiss was electrifying. Hot as hell. It was downright fucking erotic.

I was no fucking virgin, but I had never been kissed for real. Not by a man who wasn't simply taking what he wanted because he'd paid some asshole for the pleasure. I knew that's not what Cash was doing. He was just proving to me that I'm a coward, which I already knew. Still, the kiss turned me on more than I wanted to admit even to myself. My body was on fire, aching with need, and if he wanted me to, I'd probably drop down on my knees right now and let him do what he wanted. What they *always* wanted.

Except Cash wasn't like other men, and he pulled back. "Damn, Minx, I didn't expect that," he panted, eyes glazed over with lust and bewildered. "You let me know, Minx, tonight as a beginning?" He turned away and I felt a pang of sadness, maybe disappointment. But why?

"Cash."

"Yeah?" He turned a blank expression on his face.

"Tonight, and one date. I make no promises."

His mouth curled into a sexy boyish smile that made his dimples pop and his feet began to move. "I don't need promises, Minx, just a chance."

I must be crazy.

KB Winters

Chapter One

Cash

Sitting in a beat-up old pickup truck hours after the sun had already called it quits for the day, I was sweaty and tired. And ready to get some food and go home. I'd spent the past eight hours in this fucking truck watching the border to make sure former CAOS members, Wagman and Rocky, kept their shit out of Brently. We couldn't ban them outright, not yet anyway, but I knew the shit that went down at the clubhouse a few months back wasn't over. Not yet.

Rocky had served with Toro in Panama when the US government wanted Noriega gone, and I knew he had a hard-on for revenge. But what Toro had done, he fucking deserved to meet the Outlaw. I couldn't blame Rocky, hell I respected him for it. But that didn't mean I would step aside and let him fuck up my club or my town because him and his boys went against the grain. No fucking way.

But there were no signs of those assholes today. I knew they were doing business with the cartels, transporting drugs, maybe weapons and girls, from Mexico and right through Brently. That's the part I found unacceptable which was why I'd been out here most nights lately to keep an eye on things.

But tonight's shift was over, so I headed to Black Betty's to refuel. Inside I smiled when my gaze landed on the chocolate-haired beauty who's been taking up way too much of my mind space. Minx sat alone in a booth, eating and reading something on her tablet. Damn, she was just beautiful with thick brown hair and caramel highlights, big brown eyes that held a vulnerability she'd hate to know I could see, and her lush mouth seemed fixed in permanent sad face.

She had the kind of body women paid good money for. Slim but with enough meat on her bones that a man knew she was a woman, not a little girl. Her tits were more than a handful which was perfect for me since I was a breast man. Long tan legs were always on display, and sexy ass cowgirl boots were all she wore. Our night together had been amazing.

CASH

She'd been responsive as hell, and some days I got hard just thinking about it. But she still owed me a date, and I planned to cash in on it. If she thought avoiding me would make me forget, she didn't know me very well. That was something else I was determined to change.

"Long time no see," I told her, sliding into the seat across from her without waiting for the invitation I knew she wouldn't give.

She looked up, deep brown eyes looking mildly annoyed, and shook her head. "Not true. I saw you two nights ago at the clubhouse."

Yeah, there was a party to welcome the new batch of prospects, and she'd been tapped to tend bar as usual. Only something had been different that night. She didn't smile and act friendly with the guys, she kept everyone at a distance. Me included. She didn't talk to anyone more than necessary, just made their drinks and moved on. "Not really what I meant. What's up with you?"

She shrugged. "Life. Work. Not much really. You?"

I told her I've just been busy with club shit because that much was true. "How have you been?"

"I'm fine. You don't have to worry about me turning into a crazy stalker."

I kind of wished she would, goddammit. Not a stalker, of course, but at least show a little more interest. Maybe pursue me a little. "I'm not worried about that," I told her in a way that prompted a response.

"Then what are you worried about, Cash?"

"I'm worried that you're not a woman of your word. I've given you two months to come to me, Minx, but you've been avoiding me."

"Hiya, Cash," Nadine cooed, interrupting us. "What can I getcha?"

Nadine was a little too desperate for my tastes, but she was nice enough so I treated her right. "How's

CASH

it going, Nadine? I'll have the fried chicken meal with corn, potatoes, and salad."

"You eating here?" She looked between me and Minx, trying to figure out our relationship. *Good luck, sweetheart, because I don't even know.*

"Nah. Make it to go for me, would ya?"

"You got it." She winked and flounced away. I was sure if I looked she'd have a wicked swing to her hips, but my attention was squarely on Minx.

"I'm not avoiding you. I have a life to live."

"And a date you're trying to get out of." I stood and seared her with a gaze. "If you're backing out, say so. If not, I expect to hear from you soon about your availability." I figured she'd had enough of my company and went to chat with Talon, looking massively pregnant behind the counter.

Minx

I watched Cash chat with Talon while the kitchen made his meal, and then he was gone. His long powerful strides took him further away from me, and I wanted to go after him. To call him back and apologize for my constant bitchery. But I couldn't. I couldn't risk letting him get too close to me after that mind-blowing night we had together. It had been too much. Too explosive, too right, and too overwhelming for me to do that again and keep my emotions out of it. And with my past, the last thing I could afford was to form an emotional attachment to someone who might be dead in six months.

But dammit, I really, really wanted him again.

The problem was...*Cash*. He was one of those guys who was just so good, he was almost unbelievable. He held doors open for women and old people, said thank you to his servers, smiled and offered a greeting to everyone he met. And in bed, he'd shown me just how good sex could really be, and that was dangerous. I'd had plenty of sex in my life, and I knew logically that not all sexual encounters were nonconsensual and vicious, but Cash was much more than that.

So much more.

He was tender and commanding, gentle and enthusiastic. He took his time, and made sure we both had a good time. He'd even prioritized my pleasure above his own, making sure I came at least twice before he would let himself go. That had been a welcome surprise. An intoxicating encounter that, even now, had me squeezing my thighs together and talking my body down from the edge.

The edge of trouble and desire.

I had to shake off thoughts of Cash and get back to my reading. I couldn't be distracted by any man because I had a life to get back on track. After everything I'd been through, I refused to let another man be the cause of my stagnation. I needed to make plans to get away from CAOS, maybe even away from Brently. Though he saved me, things weren't the same without Magnus' smiling face. Sure, the guys at CAOS had been good to me, but it just wasn't the same.

Part of it was that I wasn't the same. Magnus had made me get my GED which I insisted be done in secret, and with that, I enrolled in a few online courses at UC San Diego. I had no idea what I'd do with a degree, if I ever got one, but I knew I needed more practical business knowledge if I wanted to do more than sew and bartend.

Yeah, things were looking up.

I could believe that too—as long as I didn't devote too much head space to a sexy biker who had me weak in the knees.

Talon sat sideways in the booth because her belly was too big to sit in it properly. "What did you say to Cash? I think you might've hurt his feelings."

I scoffed, "Doubtful. I think he was just checking to make sure I didn't turn stalker-bitch on him." Why I lied to Talon, I didn't know. She was the only person I'd willingly told about my past.

CASH

"You mean the night he rocked your world and made you walk funny for a month?" Her lips twitched, and I wanted to reach over and tug on her pigtails. "Honey, I think he's the one eager for a second night. And a third. A fourth. Fifth."

"Okay, I get it. Stop." I had to shake my head at her because now that she was blissfully in love with a baby on the way, she saw stars and romance everywhere. "I'm on a mission. Cash did what I needed him to do and I had a great time, but I can't get lost in a man right now. Or ever."

She frowned. "You don't see me getting lost, do you? There are some women who can have a man beside them *while* they conquer the world, Minx, and you're the biggest badass I know, so what's this really about?"

I sighed knowing I'd have to tell her at least some of the truth. "Maybe that's true for some women, Talon, but mentally I'm basically a teenage girl in terms of experience. I can't turn boy crazy while I'm trying to get my life squared away. Seek out a future for myself."

Like a real friend, she ignored most of what I said and focused on the important things. "Tell me about these goals," she asked, her silver eyes sparkling with curiosity.

I sucked in a long, fortifying breath and told her about school, preparing for laughter though I knew Talon wouldn't laugh at me—or my goals. "Shhh. Keep it down," I told her when she squealed "No one else knows, and I want to keep it that way." I didn't know why I was making such a big deal out of it, but it was my secret to keep, and that meant something to me. *Little things.*

"My lips are sealed." She promised and pushed off the booth to wrap me in another hug. "Even though you don't need it, I want you to know I'm proud of you."

"Thanks, Talon." She'd become the best friend I'd ever had just like her dad was the best man I'd ever met. She was my first real friend in my new life, my

CASH

new adult life. Not that I didn't love Charlie, Magnus' old lady, but after the truth came out about his death, she didn't come around as much and I couldn't say I blamed her. But it served as a reminder that the people I needed always left.

By force or by choice, they ended up gone.

***

Few things in this life felt better than having a day off work. It was the perfect time to run daytime errands, to take my time and just enjoy life. Having an entire week off was troubling to me, though. I knew they needed to do a bunch of super-secret shit with the prospects and they didn't want me around, but I was also pretty sure that once they had a full roster of guys again, I'd be out of a job. It was probably the push I needed to either make a go of my online clothing store or find something else to do. I definitely didn't dream of spending my life serving drinks to a crowd of rough bikers, their ol' ladies, and the *pass arounds*. No thank you.

They were nice enough guys, but I knew firsthand just how poorly rough dudes and booze mixed. Most of them were pussycats when they didn't need to be hellions, but there were a few—some gone and some not—I made sure never to be alone with. Though that probably had more to do with my own issues than them as men.

Cash though, I avoided being alone with for tons of other reasons. The man was everywhere—at the diner, the clubhouse. In my dreams. "Damn man," I grumbled and stepped from my vintage VW van when I arrived at the fabric store a few towns over in Clarity. I'd spotted a few good deals online that made me certain the drive was worth it, especially because one of them would become a maternity dress for Talon. The woman owned at least a hundred sundresses, and now she couldn't wear them. The indigo and lavender floral pattern would look stunning against her fairy eyes and raven hair. Fabric stores were like a world of beauty to me. I could look at a bolt of fabric and see what I could be, how it could be used to maximized the best things about it from cut to weight to quality.

For years I wore little more than cheap lingerie, but out here I found a love for passion that was possibly the only thing about me that remained from my childhood. What little there was of it. So, I'd spent the past year trying to make a go of it online, which explained why the older woman who owned Fabric City smiled when she rang me up. "Thanks, Mae."

"No problem, honey. Any chance I could get you to make me something?"

"Name the style and the fabric."

Mae pointed a finger at me, skin blushing furiously. "I'm not young and sexy like you, Minx, so I'll find the fabric if you promise to make me look good."

"You have my word, Mae."

"Then I'll see you soon."

I nodded and walked out to the sounds of my hungry stomach protesting its empty state. In my zeal to get the day started, I got up, got dressed, and headed out to run errands. As I put my purchases in my van, I considered heading to the taco place that was calling my name from a few doors down.

"Minx?"

I froze at the sound of my name, but my heart raced at the sound of the familiar voice calling it. I knew that voice, but dammit I'd driven two towns and nearly an hour away just to avoid him or anyone else I knew. *Double damn.* But Cash had seen me, and called out to me, so I couldn't pretend I didn't hear him. As much as I wanted to do just that. I turned around and plastered on my best fake smile. "Cash. Fancy seeing you out here. Taking advantage of the sale on fabric?" I motioned toward the fabric shop.

A small smile touched his lips, and instantly I thought about all the wicked things his mouth had done to me. Things no mouth had ever done to me, and I smiled in response. "Not exactly. A friend is fixing the seat of my bike. What are you doing all the way out here?"

CASH

"Buying fabric. Having lunch. Enjoying a day off." Days off actually, but knowing Cash, he might try to do something about it.

"Sure, Minx, I would love to join you for lunch." He took a step forward so we stood shoulder to shoulder and slung a heavy arm around me. He kept his pace set to my slower one. "Tacos sound good to you, too?"

I bumped his hip and rolled my eyes. "That's where I was heading, yes." I should be terrified being so close to him like this, when he topped me by at least six inches and probably close to one hundred pounds, but I wasn't. Which said a lot about just how much he threw me off my game. "Join me if you must."

He laughed. "Now how can I possibly turn down an invitation issued with such enthusiasm?"

I shrugged. "I guess you can't." His laughter filled the restaurant as he held the door open for me. "Such a gentleman."

"Just how my mama raised me." He grinned and flashed those damn dimples that never hesitated to make my panties wet. Just a little. Okay, a lot.

"Lucky you." I hadn't seen my own mother in so long that I just stopped thinking about her and the family I used to have. The moment I realized that my overly religious family would probably compound what I'd gone through by rejecting me or worse, trying to fix me. I hoped they believed I was dead because it meant no one would come looking for me, and I could just stop talking about my past. Hell, I'd give anything if I could stop thinking about it.

"What do you want, Minx?"

I blinked and looked up to see a pretty Mexican waitress and Cash staring at me with concerned eyes. "Oh, um, I'll have three fish tacos with extra guac, and a tall margarita on the rocks"—Cash looked at me with smiling eyes that shone with surprise— "and fresh chips and salsa please."

"Healthy appetite," he said once the waitress was gone.

CASH

"Is that a problem?"

"Not at all. I love a woman who loves to eat." He winked and sipped his water as if he hadn't just put a dirty image in my mind. Like I often did when it came to Cash, I ignored the part of his statement I didn't want to deal with.

"I doubt that. You strike me as the kind of guy who loves petite girls that nibble on salad as you regale them with the dangerous antics of a former SEAL while chomping on a big juicy steak."

He laughed and dammit he looked so sexy, so inviting when his face softened in laughter. All the stress lines of years in battle disappeared, leaving him a devastating mess of blond hair, dimples, and glittering emerald eyes. "I would never presume to tell a woman what to order. If you ordered a taco salad I *would* judge you, but only silently."

I couldn't help the laughter that bubbled up out of me at his witty words. Despite the intensity I always spotted in him, he was a goofball with a wicked sense of humor. "I can handle your judgment," I snapped. I was used to being judged.

"So, Minx,"—he sat back casually, a soothing smile on his face— "tell me about yourself."

My gaze narrowed, and my bullshit detector rose. "What do you want to know?" I had no real experience dealing with men on a personal level like this other than the club, and those guys treated me like a little sister so I was out of my depth. Cash was foreign territory for me.

"Where are you from for starters?"

"I lived in Terre Haute before...everything."

"Have you been back since you left?"

Since I left? He said it like I just moved away. "Nope."

"Okay. Well how did you end up in Brently?"

I slammed my glass down, bullshit meter beeping like crazy now, and glared at him. "Seriously? Are you for real right now?" It was the worst kept secret in

CASH

Brently, how Magnus rescued me and helped me get on my feet.

"I believe I am serious and for real," he said cautiously like I was the crazy one who might lash out at any moment. "Should I know this information already?"

My brows furrowed in confusion. "The CAOS guys gossip liked old ladies, so how could you not know?"

He shook his head. "I asked Mick what your deal was, and he said to ask you. I tried Talon, and she said the same thing. So I'm asking you."

I knew I could tell Cash the cold hard truth about my past and end this flirtation right now. He would look at me the way everyone else did once they knew. Like I was spun glass that required delicate handling. Like I was a bird with a broken wing. They didn't sympathize with me—they pitied me, and I fucking hated that. "If you don't know about my past, why are you always trying to help me? Fix me?"

31

He looked shocked. "Do I do that?"

"Feels like it," I shot back honestly.

"I'm sorry about that, Minx." He shrugged, not looking all that sorry. "I'm a man, a soldier, and a gentleman. If I see a woman carrying bags, it's second nature to offer to carry them for her, to hold open doors, and offer help. If you want me to back off just say so. Don't avoid me."

"And you will? Back off?"

"I'll try," he replied with that devilish smile that said he wouldn't try all that hard.

I sighed, grateful for the arrival of my margarita. "This isn't the time to tell you. Maybe another time when we're not in public."

He leaned forward. "Will there be a time we're together in a place that isn't so public?"

"Maybe. Depends."

"On what," he asked, lips curled into a smug grin. He was so sure I wanted him, and the fact that I did only made his smile annoy me more.

CASH

"Whether or not you eat like a farm animal." He laughed and tossed a warm tortilla chip at me, which I promptly caught in my mouth. "Thanks."

"Neat trick."

"Jealous?"

Cash leaned back in his chair and slung one arm across the empty space beside him as he took a sip of his beer, his eyes never left mine. "Never been jealous of a tortilla chip a day in my life. Until now."

I pressed my thighs together under the table to stop the building, swelling ache between them and bit back a groan.

Then the gorgeous bastard laughed.

Damn him.

Chapter Two

Cash

Fucking Wagman had been burning up the road between Brently and Tacapeo for the past few days, and I knew he was up to no good. I watched that fucker slip across the border and back at least six times in the past three days, and every time his saddlebags were full to bursting. To anybody paying attention it would look as though a member of CAOS was doing the transporting, and I knew that shit was intentional. But I couldn't do a damn thing about it because he wore an all-black leather vest with no club insignia.

I followed on my Ducati just in case I found myself in a sticky situation and needed a fast getaway. Hogs were nice, reliable, All-American bikes. But this bad boy was built for speed and precision. It was a perfect stakeout vehicle. I kept a distance between us because I knew I could catch up if I needed to—for

CASH

now I just wanted to observe. And I did. I watched him bypass the unmarked entrance to one of Lazarus' stash houses and drive another twenty miles to another stash house used by the Mexican Devils. This house was situated on the border of Ozo and Clarity, which meant he had technically broken the rules.

But watching him take cash from a young Devil I'd never seen before, I knew he was still doing dirty shit. Those packages were almost certainly drugs because the Devils were deep into heroine and coke. Legal weed across the country had put them out of the green business, and there were whispers of sex trafficking, but not even the Feds had been able to prove it. Not yet, anyway.

I hopped back on my bike and drove toward Brently, pulling over at a truck stop to update Mick. "Yeah, Wagman was by himself, but he went over the border to pick up the packages he dropped off in Clarity."

"Shit! All right, good going, Cash. Now get your ass back here, and be careful."

"Got it." I shoved the phone in my pocket and pulled back onto the road, eating up the cement that would carry me home at dangerous speeds. Driving the Ducati meant I had to travel light, only two pieces, but it also gave me tremendous speed.

In my rearview I could see two bikes gaining on me, one of them belonged to Wagman. *Shit*. I hoped they hadn't made me, but just in case I pressed hard on the gas and put a lot more distance between us. I was strapped, always was as a former soldier, but why risk it when it was safer to outrun them?

This time.

But Wagman and his buddy had the fires of hell powering their bikes and caught up to me, crisscrossing behind me and in front of me in an attempt to disorient me. But I'd been in worse situations with worse odds and unlike these old bastards, I was fresh from years as a SEAL and had youth on my side.

In front of me, Wagman looked back with a sneer and pulled out that weak ass black pistol he was

CASH

always twirling around his fingers. With less than a second to make a decision, I pressed the gas and knocked against his back tire just as he got two shots off and skidded to a stop after about a quarter mile. The asshole kept shooting, but lucky for me, Wagman was a shitty shot. Always had been and now when he needed to be better. He wasn't.

The other guy slowed to a stop beside Wagman, and I finally caught a glimpse of the devil horns tattooed on his forehead identifying him as a member of the Mexican Devils. He didn't even glance my way, so I turned the bike around and took off like a motherfuckin' rocket. *Brently here I come.*

The last thing I felt like was hanging around a bunch of men, but I needed to stop at the clubhouse to debrief with Roddick and Mick. It amazed me how, in just a few short months, Mick had taken his VP role and made it mean something. Like the debriefing, it took us all back to what we'd been trained to do by the U.S. government. Though we all had our own reasons for leaving the service, Mick made us all realize we should take the good we learned and apply it.

It took ten minutes for the full debrief which included a map from memory of the drop house location in Ozo. "There was a Mexican Devil with him. Asshole didn't draw his weapon or even look my way."

Roddick grinned. "Good. They're just using him as transport which means he and Rocky are on their own. No back up from the cartel. Thanks, Cash, good job."

I accepted the clap on the back and a CAOS handshake from both men before I booked it out of the clubhouse. I loved that place, but sometimes a man just wanted to be alone. Or mostly alone, I amended after I stopped by Black Betty's for two dinners, picked up a bottle of Jameson, and headed toward the little cottage in town Minx rented. She might be furious. I never knew what would piss off the little firecracker, but tonight I willingly risked it.

CASH

She pulled open the door and frowned. "What are you doing here?" She didn't seem upset just confused.

But goddamn she looked so fucking sexy in tight red shorts and a matching tank that highlighted every single one of her dangerous curves. Her toes were painted silver with two rings on one toe, and fuck me she smelled like she'd showered with rose petals. Everything about her was soft and smooth and delicate. Sharp contrast considering her sharp tongue. "I came to see you," I told her with the smile that made most women swoon. When that didn't happen, I held up my loot. "And I brought dinner."

She took a step back and grinned. "Next time lead with the food." Walking down the short hall that looked to be the living room, she looked over her shoulder. "Take off your shoes."

My eyes were glued to the round shape of her ass, looking like a question mark in profile, and I couldn't stop staring. I knew she'd said something, but had no idea what. "Were you getting ready for bed?"

"No, why?"

"No reason." Except my cock strained so hard against the zipper I knew I'd be sporting those teeth as imprints for at least a week.

"Come on in if you're staying and lock the door."

"Is that an invite?" I bit back a smile because even though Minx was a hard-ass and short with most people, I could tell she liked me. Even if she didn't want to.

"Do you need one?" she asked, eyebrows raised and hands on her hips.

"No." Letting me in was as close to an invitation as I would likely get, and I understood that.

"Well then," she answered and disappeared into the kitchen, leaving me to kick off my boots and follow after her. "I hope one of those meals is fried chicken," she warned as she gathered dishes and silverware. "If not, you get water."

"I brought my own drink," I told her with a smirk as I showed off my bottle of Jameson.

CASH

"Not if one of these isn't friend chicken, you didn't." Arms crossed she dared me, and I was so tempted to unscrew the cap and take a long swig. Instead, I pulled the Styrofoam containers from the plastic bag and flipped them open at the same time.

"Fried fish and chicken. I figured we could split it."

Minx cocked an eyebrow, lips pursed together in an effort not to smile. But she wanted to, I could tell. She liked control of her world, and I was messing that up. "In that case, you can have *ice* water."

I laughed at her tough words as she pulled two bottles of beer from the fridge and opened them before handing one to me. "Thanks for dinner. I couldn't imagine cooking in this dreadful heat."

"You could have had food delivered."

She frowned. "I don't do that."

I could feel the frown form on my face and I tried to get rid of it, but she'd already seen it and gave me one in return. "You don't have food delivered. Why?"

"I don't like strangers showing up at my door." She said it with such a blank expression I knew I had to be missing something.

Obviously that didn't include me because she'd let me in, and I couldn't deny the small measure of pride I felt at that knowledge. "Smart for a woman living alone, even a tough one. I'm guessing there's a reason you aren't going to share with me behind that rule?"

Big brown eyes assessed me for a long, uncomfortable moment. She had a way with those vulnerable liquid brown eyes that made me feel like a hero returning from battle and a speck of dirt on her shoe at the same time. I wondered which she leaned toward now. "Not that I'm not appreciative, but what brings you by?"

I guess we're changing the subject. "Some shit went down earlier, and I wanted to see a friendly face."

"Yet you chose my face instead?"

CASH

"Aw, Minx," I joked with a charming smile, "you're mostly friendly. When you want to be. Besides, I like looking at your face." The blush that flooded her cheeks took me by surprise. I couldn't remember the last time I saw any woman blush, never mind one as tough as Minx. But the more I knew her the more I glimpsed someone softer. Vulnerable.

She looked up and her gaze slammed right into mine. "Right back atcha, Cash."

I knew she was uncomfortable so I leaned forward and batted my eyelashes, making her life. "Why thank you, Minx. A man does love to hear how irresistible a beautiful woman finds him."

Her lips twitched, but I was learning to realize that Minx came by her seriousness honestly. "Why did you need to see a friendly face?"

She switched topics at speeds fast enough to give a man whiplash. "Club shit," was all I answered, expecting her to ask a thousand questions I couldn't answer. Instead, she nodded and took a long pull from the water-coated beer bottle.

"Are you okay?"

"Pissed off and shaken up, but good food and good company helps."

Minx raised her bottle to me with a grin before taking another sip and drawing my gaze to those naturally plump lips that gave me an instant hard on. Abruptly, she stood and began clearing the table in silence. She didn't look upset or angry, but I guessed that was my cue to leave. I was about to stand when she turned with two shot glasses and a smile. "Making things fuzzy tends to help, at least in my experience." Then she sauntered off into another room, leaving me to follow her.

Again. She never failed to surprise me. As tough and badass as she appeared, she blushed easily and had a soft spot she hid from the world. "Thank you."

She nodded and held up her shot glass, both shaped and colored like avocados. I filled them both, and she tapped the edges with a grin and knocked it back while I did the same. We repeated those motions like an old married couple two more times before she finally spoke. "I'm not what you think I am."

"I don't think you're anything in particular. Well, except hot as fuck and prickly as hell."

She smiled, but this time it didn't reach her eyes. Instead, they were far off. Cold. Distant. "I don't need to be saved."

"I'm not in the business of saving people who don't need it. That's why I left the Navy."

"Good." She gave a proud nod as though we'd settled something.

"Minx?"

"Cash," she responded in a breathy whisper that sent a spear of fire right to my cock. Left me pulsing and aching to bury myself in her. But I wouldn't.

For now, I just wanted something simple. "I wanna kiss you, sweetheart."

She nodded but I was already descending, her pretty face growing closer and closer until our mouths touched. I swept inside and she allowed it, tasting me as fervently as I tasted her. We kissed like horny teenagers making out on the sofa, letting our hands explore each other's bodies. She was soft and silky everywhere I was hard, sharp edges.

When she slid onto my lap, I worried I might lose my shit. In those tiny ass shorts my hands gripped her tight, but the warmth of her pussy was so hot I felt it through my jeans as she ground against me. Back and forth her hips moved along the length of my cock, and I knew we were at the point where we either stopped—or moved forward.

And damn, I wanted to move forward.

Her hands slid under my shirt, stroking my muscles to distraction before she finally got rid of the damned thing. "So hot," she moaned and pressed kisses from my collarbone to my abs.

"Your turn," I told her and pulled the tank from her body, putting those magnificent tits right in my

CASH

face. Close enough to taste them. I grabbed them both in my hands and flicking my tongue against the tight, dusky pink tips before pulling them into my mouth. God, she was so sweet and so fucking responsive, I could smell her arousal already. I slipped a hand into those red shorts and holy fuck, she coated my fingers with her juices. "Minx," I groaned as she held my head close to her tits, urging me on.

Her response was to grind against my hand, gaze pinned to mine in an intense look that tightened my balls. "Yes," she moaned low and deep, stealing all of my control with another small move of her hips. Her hands flew to my waistband, unfastening my belt and my pants with an urgency that told me our kisses had affected her as much as me. "Cash."

"Tell me."

"I want you."

"Then have me, sweetheart." At my words, she reached inside my boxer briefs and gripped my cock. Her gaze never left mine as she stroked me from balls to tip. "Minx."

She stood and pushed the red shorts down her legs before kicking them away. Climbing back on my lap she wasted no time coating my cock with the slick juices that flooded her thighs. "Condom," she groaned, and I reached for my pocket and produced one.

Biting back every impulse I had, I let her roll the rubber down my cock and secure it in place. "You're killin' me, babe."

Her hands rested on the sofa behind my head as she balanced above my erect cock that searched for her cunt like a heat-seeking missile. "Ahh, but what a way to go, right?" She gripped me and impaled herself on my cock, letting out a cry so throaty and erotic I had to dig my fingers into her flesh to stop the urge to come. "Cash," she moaned my name over and over again as she slid up and down my shaft, fucking me like her life depended on it.

I kept hold of her hips so I could thrust up in her as our skin grew slick with our efforts. The sound of flesh smacking hard only made my desire stronger, my need for her out of control. Harder and harder I thrust while she rode my cock, bouncing and swiveling her hips in a way that tantalized me. "Cash," she groaned in warning, and I slid a hand between us, rubbing her clit in fast circles to ratchet up her pleasure until she exploded around my cock. She convulsed in my arms as the orgasm washed over her. "Yes. Oh, God, Cash! Yes!"

That was all I needed to hear to let myself go and pound into her dripping cunt until my own orgasm ripped out of my body on a loud roar. I fell back on the sofa and she sank onto me, pulling me deeper inside her wet, still pulsing body. "Minx, you've wrecked me."

She laughed and laid her head on my shoulder. "That was some kiss."

I did the only thing I could in that moment. I laughed.

***

Minx

One of my favorite things about living on my own was waking up, even if it was to an annoying fucking alarm clock. It was better than the screams, rock music, or the sounds of someone fucking. Last night I'd slept more peacefully than I had in ages, probably since what ended up being my last night in my childhood home. But when I woke, groggy from exertion, I panicked at the feel of the hot, hard, and obviously male body pressed against mine. I tried to move, to slide out of bed, but strong arms kept me close.

I would have screamed my fool head off too, if his arms hadn't relaxed and he hadn't dropped a kiss just behind my ear. Cash. The man had the body of one of those Gods that museums loved to depict naked. Of course, I hadn't been to a museum in a long time, but I remembered how they looked, tall and wide, masculine. They were all man, just like Cash. He

CASH

smelled like sin and sex and something uniquely male, and just like that my body began to relax.

What was it about this man that slipped under my defenses? That made me relax when I should be on guard? I didn't know, but I knew he was dangerous. A guy like Cash had the power to make me do the one thing I vowed never to do when I was free. Wish for things I couldn't have. I gasped at the feel of his thumb and forefinger applying pressure to my nipple and instantly felt desire flood my insides.

The man had to be a magician, that was the only explanation for how he'd gotten me to sleep with him. Twice. How could I so easily fall into bed with him as if the past hadn't happened to me? As if it didn't loom over me every fucking day like a perpetual black cloud. I let out a long sigh to get rid of the thoughts that came far too early in the morning. The sun hadn't even risen yet, but my mind was running a marathon already.

"That is the loudest thinking I've ever heard. Don't tell me you woke up with morning after regrets?"

"Only that we didn't get to try that thing we talked about," I answered honestly.

"Next time," he promised and dropped a kiss on my shoulder.

"Cash, there can't be a next time."

He went stiff and pulled back. "You said that last time, Minx. Will I have to wait another two months until your itch needs to be fucked?"

"I told you I wasn't ready for this!" I scrambled out of bed and walked naked across the room to grab my robe. "I like this," I told him as I pointed between our bodies. "Hell, I even like you, Cash, but I'm not ready. Not for this. Not yet." I heard the wobble in my voice, and fucking hated it. I didn't like anyone to see me vulnerable because I never knew who'd use that against me in the future. That went double for men who would exploit that weakness for their own depraved needs.

CASH

"You keep saying that, but I don't know what it means. Or why you're not ready, Minx. You're a grown woman, goddammit!"

That was the problem. On the outside, I was a grown woman, but on the inside, I was still a girl. "It means I don't know what I'm doing, Cash, and until I do, I won't risk it."

His expression turned dark. "But you can fuck me when the mood strikes you?"

I reeled back as though he'd slapped me. I never realized his words could hurt so much. Hell, more than any fist I'd ever taken, and I'd taken plenty of fists. Feet, a flashlight, a lamp and even the butt of a gun. They all hurt like hell, but not like this. "I...you...," My words wouldn't come, so I took a moment to gather myself and pushed my emotions way down. "No, I can't. I'm sorry. Goodbye, Cash." I swiped a tear from my eye and fled to the bathroom, staying there until I heard his angry steps to the living room to retrieve his clothes and then out the door.

Once I was sure he was gone, I got dressed for the day, washed my bedding, and started on my homework. I had shit to do, a future to plan. I didn't have time to spend hours thinking about the green-eyed cutie who'd shown me how great sex could be. I couldn't think about him or his angry words or else I might do something stupid, like call him up and beg him to come back.

That means explaining why you're not ready, the logical part of my brain reminded me. So I dug back in to my homework, highlighting and making notes before I finally finished my paper due at the end of the week.

With hours still left in my day, I decided to finish Talon's dress so I could get started on a few new designs I'd started last week. The second bedroom doubled as my sewing studio and I spent hours in there, hunched over the machine and then the drawing table I'd found at Goodwill.

It was secondhand like most of the things in my little rental cottage, but I still loved it. With just two bedrooms, the house was more than I needed, but it turned out to be perfect for me. I'd decorated it in vibrant colors, yellow and red for the kitchen, blue and green in the small living room, and shades of gold for my bedroom. All the little embellishments, pillows and blankets, I made myself.

And I was proud to say I didn't spend the whole day thinking about Cash. By the time I curled up in front of the television, I had only thought about him about three times an hour.

So, yeah. Progress.

Chapter Three

Minx

Driving and having my own van was one of my true pleasures in life. Magnus had told me, "A girl with the capability to drive always has an escape route. Even if you need to beg, borrow, and steal to get a ride, once you have it you'll know what to do it with." Coming from that big burly man, the words struck a chord. And every time I put my ass in the driver's seat I thought of his words and the power a driver's license had given me. It meant that each time I got behind the wheel I was choosing to come back home.

Today I wasn't really *choosing,* but I had to drive up to San Diego because my business ethics course—surprise, surprise—required all students to show up for the test. In person. What the hell good was taking online courses if they could still summon you far and wide, I didn't know. But the test was over, and I was

CASH

pretty sure I kicked ass despite my shitty test taking skills. Knowing I'd mastered most of the material left me feeling confident, and that made for a relaxing ride back to Brently.

Even though I didn't enjoy the long drive, I did enjoy the scenery that seemed to switch between lush green grass and water so blue it almost looked fake, and dry swaths of golden earth. Both gave me the kind of relaxation that comes from familiarity, from looking at a place and knowing right where I was. The first few times I drove by myself I felt panic set in at the idea that I didn't know where I was going or how to get back to Brently even though Magnus had given me a GPS.

Now I didn't have that problem. It turned out, I had a damn good sense of direction, pretty ironic if you asked me. But helpful and it was a skill I tested regularly.

The day started so well that I should have known it wouldn't stay that way. I got to school and found a parking spot, I did well on the test, and the drive home was relaxing. At least until about an hour outside of Brently when my van coughed, choked, and then died in spectacular fashion. "Damn you!" I smacked the steering wheel in frustration, but it was my own fault. Magnus told me this old van was a piece of crap, but I had to have it. And now I was stuck between two towns in the hot desert heat. I needed help, and I had only a few options.

Talon was too pregnant to do that much driving, so I wouldn't even ask her. I would have called Charlie, but she'd left a few days ago to take a cruise, to get away from reminders of CAOS and the man the club had stolen from her too soon. That meant I had to use my AAA service which was fine, it was exactly why I paid the damn fees every year. I made the call and climbed back in the van to at least avoid sunburn and dehydration.

No sooner had I settled in with an audio book on my phone did I hear the roar of a motorcycle. It was a sound I had gotten used to over the past few years, but it always caused a rise in my anxiety. I waited for it to pass but when it didn't I went on alert, scanning

CASH

my mirrors to see where the bike had gone and more importantly, who it belonged to. I nearly jumped out of my seat when a knock sounded on the passenger window.

Cash.

"You gonna roll down the window or what?"

"Or what," I answered like a child.

"Car trouble?"

"Not once AAA arrives." The nice woman on the phone said forty-five minutes. I could listen to a few chapters until then.

"Damn. I'm right here Minx. I can give you a ride home." He smiled but I could tell he was frustrated with me, probably because he thought I was playing games, but I really wasn't.

"Thanks for the offer, but I'll wait. I don't want to leave my van here unattended." That was part of the reason, anyway.

"Fine. I'll wait with you and then you can let me take you out to dinner." He flashed that panty-melting smile, and I squeezed my knees together, refusing to be moved by his gorgeous smile or those laughing eyes.

"No thanks. I have no itch that needs to be fucked," I said pointedly.

He groaned and smacked the roof with his palm. "Dammit, Minx."

Exactly what I had expected. Anger, not an apology. He probably didn't owe me one because he didn't understand why I wasn't ready, but my stupid emotions didn't get the memo, and they were well and truly offended. "You've done your duty by offering, Cash, so thank you." Leaning against the headrest, I closed my eyes and hoped he would go away though I knew that was unlikely. Despite his harsh words to me last week, he was a good man.

"It's not duty, Minx."

"All the more reason for you to continue on your journey home."

CASH

I heard the heavy footfalls of his boots walk away, but I realized he wanted me to hear him walk away. Any other time the man moved with the stealth of a ninja, but now he sounded like an old woman with a cane and a bad cough. I waited but the loud roar of the motorcycle never came. He was still here.

Damn him.

Finally, the AAA driver arrived and hooked my van up to the tow, promising it would end up at Mick's place just as I had requested. "You got a ride?"

"If you could just take—"

"Yes, she does." His words had the desired effect on the skinny gray-haired driver who shuffled back into the truck and pulled into traffic.

"I told you I don't need your help. More to the point, I don't want it."

The bastard smiled. "Well, it looks like you're stuck with it now. May as well agree to dinner, too."

"I don't need to agree to anything since you're making all the choices, do I?" *This*. This was why I'd been keeping my distance from men. This loss of control left me feeling shaken and vulnerable, two things I fucking hated more than I hated the bitch who orchestrated my kidnapping.

"Minx." I kept walking toward the bike, and he followed on my heels. "Minx, come on." He sighed heavily, but I didn't turn to face him because I didn't want him to see how close I was to losing my shit. "If that's really how you feel then."

"Then what," I asked without turning. "You've sent away the only other ride I had, so just forget it. Come on." Fifteen minutes later the bike came to a stop again. Dinner, I guessed by our location. We both dismounted the bike and headed inside the greasy spoon diner that looked like a shithole compared to Black Betty's. It was just called 'Diner', and the green pleather booths were more ripped than whole. Half the chairs were missing from the counter, and everything was covered in a layer of dirt. The thing I'd learned about these kinds of places was that they're hit or miss. Despite the shitty outside, the food might actually be good.

CASH

"Hungry?"

"I guess." We sat and Cash tried to catch my gaze, but I refused him. Not because I was mad, which I was, but because I needed to break this strange hold he had over me.

"You plan on being mad at me all night?"

I shrugged. "You're a long way from Brently out here."

He laughed and shook his head. "You know I do things other than sit around the clubhouse all day, right?"

I didn't know, actually. No one ever told me shit. Hell, lately I hadn't even been getting hours at the bar so no, I didn't know. "Like what?"

"Me and a few buddies have a partnership in a franchise of dispensaries up and down the state, and we take turns providing security for the money runs."

"An entrepreneur. Impressive." I knew some of the club guys like Mick had businesses outside the club, and I assumed they all knew this shit could fall apart at any moment. Magnus had learned that lesson the hard way.

"Does it make you more interested?"

"No. But it makes me think that maybe I misjudged you." We placed our orders with the middle-aged waitress, and I tried not to think too hard about his knees brushing against mine or the way his helmet had given him bedhead that only made him look hotter and sexier.

"You thought I was just some dumb biker"

"No." I slowly drank my tea as I searched for a way to say it without offending him. "Men who choose to join these types of organizations don't tend to do much planning for the future."

"That's true, but you forget we're all veterans. Planning has been drilled into us until it's second nature." He shrugged. "Some guys don't live that way because they hate it, but for some of us, it has become a way of life."

"Okay."

CASH

"That's it?"

"Yep." Finally, the waitress arrived with our food, burgers and fries for both of us. I dug in and moaned. "Definitely a sleeper."

"A what?"

"You know, it looks like the kind of place that will give you food poisoning, but damn this burger is amazing!" It had bacon and avocado on it with smoked gouda.

"You could still get food poisoning," he pointed out.

I froze at his words and grinned. "Totally worth it." We made quick work of our food, but still the sun was sinking in the sky when we walked out to his bike. "You guys have something against actual cars?"

He flashed that damn panty-melting smile again, and not gonna lie, those bad boys melted right off. "Wouldn't make sense for a motorcycle club to drive minivans, would it?" His lips twitched, and I bumped my hip against his.

"You're not funny."

"Yet you're smiling." He pushed me up against the pickup beside his bike with his big body shadowing out all other light. "Why is that I wonder," he brushed a kiss along one side of my jaw, then the other. "Maybe you actually like me," he whispered before nibbling my ear and kissing his way to my mouth. "Is that it, Minx, you like me?"

He didn't wait for an answer, just took my mouth in a blistering kiss that made me forget all of my reservations about him. Made me forget that we were in the middle of a parking lot on the side of the freeway. Forget that this man kissing me was a distraction. But dammit, he was deliciously distracting, doing things to my mouth that I felt in my pussy. Moments under his spell and my skin became slick. Slippery. And his hands—big and strong and compelling—never moved from my hips. He pulled back, and I knew I wore a stupid, hazy grin. "I really like doing that."

CASH

He grinned. "Me too," he responded and stepped back to help me on the bike. In no time, we were eating up the pavement toward Brently. The night air chilled my overheated skin, but a prickle of awareness washed over me, and I didn't know the cause. I'd learned years ago to listen to that instinct, and I held myself stiff and looked over my shoulder.

Nothing.

Weird. Maybe I imagined it, I thought. It wouldn't be completely odd for me to feel in danger when no danger existed, but this didn't feel like that. I looked again, and just as I turned back two sets of lights flipped on. Bike lights. "Cash,"—I patted his shoulder and shouted in his ear— "we have company."

He took a look of his own and revved the engine, throttling faster down the highway. The roar vibrated my whole body which was still on the edge from that kiss. It was a strange mixture of fear and desire that I wasn't sure I liked, but seeing as I was pressed tight against the hard body of a former SEAL, there wasn't much I could do about it. He crossed between cars on all sides, making a serpentine motion down the road to put some distance between us and the bikers giving chase. Five minutes later the lights couldn't be seen, and he slowed onto the side of the road and turned off the lights. "Shit."

"I guess you know who that was?"

He nodded as he removed the helmet. "Got a pretty good fucking idea."

Of course he did. "Club shit?" Lately there had been too much club shit going on for guys who proclaimed to be the good guys.

"Yeah."

"Okay then. Get me home please."

He nodded and climbed off the bike and walked away to make a call that lasted maybe twenty seconds, and then we were back on the road. Forty minutes later I closed and triple-locked my door behind me and let out a few calming breaths. My hands shook and my teeth chattered, only a hot tea with a shot of whiskey would do me any good, so I marched to the kitchen on autopilot.

I couldn't say for sure but I was pretty sure some bad shit was brewing—again—and I had a feeling this time, things would end with a simple club vote.

***

Cash

"Those fuckers tried to run me off the road, and I had Minx on the bike with me!" I fumed, pacing in front of the Church doors where Mick and Roddick waited for me. "They had to have been following me because I only came up on Minx by chance." I froze. "Unless they were following *her*."

Roddick stood, an imposing figure, stood broad with arms crossed and a dark scowl on his face. "No more following them on your own. Teams from here on out." He stared me down to make sure I heard him.

"Got it." Goddamn Rocky and Wagman had become a pain in my ass and the club's. Right about now I wanted to kick my own ass for not voting to get rid of them all. "They're moving drugs over the border for the Mexican Devils."

"Yeah, Dante told me they tried to sell some to his crew which is weird since the cartels don't fuck with black." Mick scratched his beard, his gaze darting between me and Roddick. "Think we should take that news to Lazarus?"

Roddick blew out a breath and scrubbed a hand down his beard. "You mean some enemy of my enemy type shit?"

He nodded. "Exactly. It would relieve us of the headache they're causing by hanging around Brently. Plus, if Lazarus finds out on his own we'll be cleaning bodies up off the streets of Brently, and then we'll have to worry about Sheriff Darlington."

I nodded. "If they're following me they might be following others, so we need to make sure everyone keeps their heads on a swivel." I was so fucking

CASH

amped up from that chase, I knew it would be hours before I came down. Knowing one of those crazy bastards could have started shooting with Minx between us made me so damn mad I didn't think I'd be able to stop myself from hunting them down and filling those assholes full of lead. "I need to get out of here," I grumbled, still pacing like a caged animal.

"Come on, let's go grab some food." Mick clapped me on my back and pushed me toward the exit. "You're too damn wound up, man."

"Minx was on the back of my bike, bro. Last time fucking Wagman let a few bullets loose." I shook my head, still fucking fuming from that shit. "I got a bullet with that motherfucker's name on it, Mick."

"If you have to, just make sure it's justified. The last thing we need right now is to start more shit with the cartel."

I knew what he was saying was right. We were still rebuilding our numbers and getting back to trusting one another again. CAOS wasn't ready for battle, and I'd be damned if I pushed us there before we were. But I had a strong urge to fuck some shit up right about now.

"So you and Minx, huh?"

I grinned as we walked into Black Betty. "She'll deny it until her dying breath, but yeah." I wanted to ask Mick about her past again because I knew she was hiding something, but for some reason, I wanted her to be the one to tell me. "Skittish as hell, though."

Mick took the booth near the back, facing the window. I didn't like having my back to the door, but I trusted Mick with my life. Had done so many times in the past, except those last three years after he'd retired. "Yeah, well, she has a good reason to be skittish. If you mistreat her, Talon will cut off your balls so...you know."

Yeah, I knew, but still I laughed at the image of his little dark-haired spitfire coming at me. "Yeah, I got it," I sighed. "But the truth is she's more likely to mistreat me," I told him. She was scared, and I knew people often struck out when they were too scared to act, which meant I needed to be careful. I liked Minx,

CASH

but settling down wasn't on my immediate agenda. "You think we're gonna end up in the shit with Wagman and Rocky?"

Mick nodded, but his answer came slower. This was why I respected Mick so much. He never made snap decisions. He thought about shit before he spoke. "They're trying to make some cash as freelancers which comes with more danger, but they know how we operate so they know how to work around us. Most important of all, those assholes want revenge."

Yeah, I knew how fucking dangerous that could be. "Who would've thought we left the middle east behind and still ended up at war?" It's not exactly how I pictured retirement, but when I left the SEALs I was lost. After a decade of structure and order and unattainable goals, my head was fucked up without it. Meeting up with Mick and CAOS had given me new goals that were doable. It had given me a purpose. I could be a badass outlaw without actually being a bad guy.

73

"Yeah, but this is the first time we've had to deal with shit like this. Some guys need more money because they're not smart enough to come up with a side hustle like the rest of us. If I didn't have the mini mart and service station, I might be more understanding."

I nodded, understanding perfectly. Years in the service with no home, no bills, and no debt meant most of us had come out with a shit ton of cash saved to invest in something when we got home. Guys like Toro and Wagman spent until they were broke and then bitched about being broke. "Still they could have taken it to Rod."

When the waitress—not Nadine thankfully—dropped off our food, we dug in and ate in silence for a few minutes. Though I had just eaten, I inhaled my club sandwich. It wasn't close to what I wanted to release this tension, but I was pretty sure it was my only option if Minx's goodbye was any clue.

"You gotta remember, Cash, some of these guys are old school. They didn't volunteer like we did, hell even like Roddick did. Coming back with what we came back with when you didn't want that shit in the first place? Breeds a fuck of a lot of resentment."

"I guess." I couldn't stay calm and think about those fuckers, so I finished off my sandwich and onion rings and ordered a beer. I needed to focus on something more compelling. Like a certain sultry brunette with more curves than a San Francisco street and big brown eyes that could drown a man if he wasn't smart enough to reach for air.

I feared I wasn't quite that smart.

KB Winters

Chapter Four

Cash

"You gonna hit me with that?" My lips twitched as I eyed the bat Minx held in her hands, a wary smile aimed my way.

"I might. You planning on making a habit of dropping by unannounced?" Despite her harsh words, she stepped back and let me in. "No food this time?"

I laughed a pulled a big white bag with a greasy, nearly clear bottom from behind me. "Rosita's okay with you?"

She nodded and pushed the door shut behind me, engaging all three locks as she always did. "If you have a burrito in there with green chile salsa, I might start liking you."

"You already like me," I told her arrogantly because we both knew it was true. She might not *want* to like me, but she did. That's why she let me in her house and why she smiled at me now, like she knew a secret the rest of us didn't. "It's okay, Minx, because I like you, too."

"Now I can die a happy woman," she put on her best Southern drawl with her hands to her chest and fluttered her lashes.

"Glad to oblige, sugar." I winked, and she yanked the bag from me and left me standing in the small foyer. "So how'd you end up doing on that test?"

She frowned at the question as she pulled small cups of condiments from the bag, then recognition dawned. "I got a solid A. Not a perfect score but pretty damn close."

"Care to share what that test was, exactly?"

She sighed and slammed one of the burritos on the table. "I've been taking online courses at UCSD, and one of my classed required an in person test. No big deal."

Seemed like a pretty big fucking deal to me, but I decided not to push. For now. "I took a few business classes before investing some money with my friends. Made me think maybe I should've gone to school instead of the military."

"You regret your time in the Navy?"

"No, but that shit doesn't go away."

She nodded like she got it, and I wondered what shit from her past stayed with her. "You're a numbers guy?" I nodded, wearing a proud grin. "Figures," she grumbled. "I work hard to get good grades, but being out of school so long means it'll probably always be hard." She froze as though she was waiting for me to ask more.

Since she started opening up to me a little more, I looked her straight in the eyes. "You gonna tell me now?"

"Maybe after dinner," was all she said and opened the first burrito. "We can split them unless you have a preference?"

My gaze darkened at the tiny scrap of clothes she wore, the way her nipples puckered under my gaze.

"I'd prefer to eat it off you, but I suppose you have objections."

She laughed. "Melted cheese and salsa? Yeah, I object."

"I don't know, girl, it could be fun."

She froze, and I waited for her sharp tongue to lash me for my words. "Maybe on *your* sheets, but I'm not cleaning it up."

Well damn, she shocked the hell out of me. I leaned back and laughed loud and hard while she stared like I'd grown another head. "Thanks for that. And I'll happily clean up anything you let me eat off you."

She kept a saucy grin on her face while we finished putting together our plates and took them into the living room, along with a bottle of tequila. She made margaritas but I was a man, I didn't drink margaritas. "Suit yourself." She shrugged and poured a glass for her then set a measly half shot of tequila in front of me.

CASH

I ate in silence while that dinky little shot mocked me. In the end, I blamed the hot salsa along with my desire to see Minx smile again on my surrender. "Fine, pour me a drink. Please." The sound of her laugh and the way her tits jiggled when she did made it all worth it. Never mind the margarita was damn good. "You make good drinks. Maybe you should get paid for it," I joked.

"Want to pay me for it?"

"Cash or credit," I asked with more than a little innuendo in my tone. I gave her a long, heated look and licked my lips. Her pulse raced as her breathing changed, a small triangle of pink peeked out of her mouth and swept across her bottom lip, pulling a groan from me. "Flesh?"

With a pronounced swallow, she picked up her refreshed glass and took a few big gulps. "You're not that irresistible, you know."

"Oh, but I am," I told her and sat back, the half empty plate on my lap. "And you want me."

She stood quietly and walked away, and I bit back a groan. Damn, the woman was prickly as fuck. I never knew which words of mine would set her off. But she turned me on, and I couldn't stop flirting with her. I opened my mouth to apologize when a very small and thin tank top landed on my head. "You're right. I do."

I was on my feet and marching after her down the hall because goddammit I couldn't get enough of her. She was a unique mixture of shy and adventurous that kept my dick hard and my mind occupied. I stepped over her shorts on my way to her room and had to stop and adjust my cock trying to press past my zipper. Yeah, I knew I would keep coming back as long as she would let me because she was fucking irresistible. "I knew it," I told her and stopped dead in my tracks at the door to her bedroom.

Minx lay on the bed with her feet up, completely naked with her head tossed back and one finger plunging into the slick heat between her legs. "You gonna join or watch?"

CASH

I swallowed. "If it's all the same to you, I'll watch first. Then join," I told her and freed my cock from his restraints, stroking it as I watched her.

"Fine by me," she moaned, and I gripped my cock tight knowing I wouldn't be able to wait too long.

KB Winters

CASH

Chapter Five

Minx

Another week off from the clubhouse made me glad that I own my little business or else I'd be in serious financial trouble. With Magnus gone there was a consensus that I didn't get paid unless I worked, which I respected, but now that work hadn't been as steady as it was, I knew I needed to step up my plans. I spent the first two days off finishing Talon's dress along with two retro style rompers. Over the next day and a half, I cut new patterns and made two new dresses with different cuts and put them up online. I offered nearly a dozen colors and sizes so all I needed to do was wait. And advertise.

Today, though, I planned to rest, maybe do a little grocery shopping and clean my house. A nice boring day that most people took for granted but always managed to make me feel a little giddy. Packing up three boxes, I stopped at the post office where I ran into Trudy. "Hey, babe. How are things?"

Her smile looked haunted, but it was real. "Good. Really good now that Dagger's fully healed." Her shoulders had finally gotten rid of the stress they'd carried around for months now.

"I'm glad to hear that." The guys had fucked him up pretty bad, leaving him with busted ribs and broken fingers, never mind all the bruises and cuts everywhere.

"Do you think Talon would mind if I stopped by? I have some things for her, but I don't want to intrude."

"Are you kidding? She's bored when she's not at the restaurant because Mick won't let her do anything but sit around wrapped in cotton. I'm headed there now, why don't we go together?"

"Oh no, that's all right. I just wanted to thank her for saving Dagger's life. He finally told me he went over there and she helped him without question." Tears pooled in her eyes. "I owe her so much. I just…"

CASH

She turned her head, looking around as if someone could hear us. "I just don't like all the bad things that happen around the club," she said, practically in a whisper.

"Come with me."

"No, that's all right. But you can take it to her. I'll wait for you in the parking lot."

I frowned but agreed. I guessed I shouldn't judge her too harshly because I might not act all that different if my man had nearly died. I shipped my packages and grabbed the cooler from Trudy before I got in the van and headed to the fabric store for some new fabric for a few patterns I had in mind. I put everything else out of my head—or at least tried to. *Cash,* my secret wish for my own little boutique. *Cash.* My future in Brently. *Cash.*

Dammit. *Cash.*

After I left the fabric store, I drove over to Talon and Mick's. I pulled up in the drive and kicked up dust with my cowgirl boots before I climbed the wooden steps and knocked.

Talon pulled the door open with a wide happy grin. "Oh perfect, you're here!" She pulled me inside and pushed me toward the kitchen. "I thought we could have lunch and look for dresses in San Diego today." She rushed around and laid out muffins, fruit, and coffee. "If I ever find a thing to wear!"

I pushed her into a chair. "Sit down somewhere, woman, before that baby falls right out of you." I dropped the bag with her new dress in it on the table and unpacked the cooler. "Wear that, I just finished it a few days ago. And this is a thank you from Trudy for saving her man's life."

Tears pooled in her eyes and I glared at her, completely uncomfortable with her hair trigger emotions. "Sorry, but you both are so sweet."

"Yeah, I'm a real lollipop," I told her. "If you stop crying, we can go shopping," I bargained with her.

"And you'll drive because I can't fit behind the wheel?"

CASH

"Of course, I will. But shouldn't we wait to look for dresses until you have less belly?"

She grinned. "No. Mick wants to get married sooner rather than later, and I'm going to surprise him with it."

Fuck, they were so sweet it made my chest ache. I shoved that shit deep down and helped my friend into the passenger seat. It took about an hour to get to the bridal store, but when we arrived, there was air conditioning and champagne we couldn't drink since Talon was pregnant and I was the designated driver.

"This is a lot more than I was thinking it would be," she whispered to me as the shop chick went to get a few dresses.

"It doesn't have to be. What kind of dress do you want?"

She shrugged. "Something simple. Off white or maybe a very light blue."

I hopped up and began rifling through wedding gowns and bridesmaid dresses until I found a few dresses that met her criteria. "Here we are. Let's get you a dressing room."

"Excuse me," the tiny blonde crept up with a frown. "You're not supposed to do that."

"Yeah, well, you're not supposed to just pick out dresses without asking the bride what she wants. We need a room. Can you help with that?"

"Yes," she huffed and rolled her eyes, but did as I asked.

I pushed Talon inside. "Holler if you need help, and don't think you're not coming out to show me every dress."

She sighed heavily, but she tried on four dresses before finding one she loved. "What do you think?"

"Beautiful." She had on a silk empire waist with a jeweled bodice. "Like a princess. A light blue princess, but still."

She laughed and pulled me in for a hug. "Thanks, Minx. You really are the best."

CASH

I turned away from her compliment because I didn't like to hear it. Probably because I wasn't used to them, but they just made me uncomfortable. "How about this for me," I asked when I spotted a strapless blue dress that was a distant cousin to her gown.

"Perfect!" She clapped happily. "Thank you for making this so easy."

"Happy to help," I told her, feeling a rush of relief when we left the den of happily ever after. We hopped back in the van, and Talon's groan told me she'd been on her feet for far too long. "All right, let's get you two home. Do you know what you're having?"

She grinned and rubbed her belly. "No, but we find out at our next appointment. I hope for a girl because I have no real experience with boys or men for that matter."

"No kidding." I had even less experience than Talon, so I understood her reservations.

"As long as he or she is healthy, I'm happy." She grinned. "Mick wants a boy because he's terrified of having a little girl."

"Considering what happened to me, I can't blame him."

"Shit, Minx, I'm sorry."

"Don't be. It's just I get why he'd be scared. You know Magnus used to say when you have a boy you just have to worry about one dick, but when you have a girl you have to worry about all the dicks."

Talon's body shook with laughter. "I hadn't thought of it like that, but now I don't think I'll be able to think about it any other way." She wiped tears and continued to laugh. "He was a great guy, wasn't he?"

"Oh yeah. He knew a lot about life. And he'd passed plenty of lessons on to me."

Talon's stomach growled and she picked up her phone, placing an order for us at Jade Dragon. "It'll be ready for us when we get back to town." She grinned.

CASH

"You have a serious food problem," I told her, and she just laughed. The woman thought about food all day, and that's when she wasn't eating it.

"It's true, and this pregnancy has given me the perfect excuse. I'll probably be in hell when I can't pig out anymore."

"You've still got time. I hear breastfeeding burns tons of calories."

"Score!" She raised her fist in the air and then screamed, "What the—"

"Fuck," I finished when I felt the van jerk forward as we were bumped from behind. A quick glance in the mirror and I saw an old sky blue pickup truck throttling toward us at a rapid speed. It looked like Rocky, his greasy brown hair hung around his face like a crackhead. "Hang on, Talon. I need to get away from these assholes, 'kay?" She nodded, but I could see the fear written on her face, and I knew then and there I wouldn't let them harm her or that baby.

"Who is it?" She tried to look over her shoulder, but he hit us again. "Ow!"

"Don't look back, T! Just hang on and protect that baby." I punched the gas pedal to speed away, the van jerking and groaning as it slowly climbed in speed. "FUCK!" I clutched the steering wheel tighter and glanced in the rearview mirror quickly before checking on Talon. "Call Mick and tell him where we are and to get here quick! We need CAOS to shake these fuckers off our asses!"

Fear laced Talon's words as she gave Mick the details of Rocky's threat. "He said they're on their way and to just stay on the path to Brently."

"Okay." I tried to stay calm, stay brave for my friend and her baby, but this latest shit with CAOS was pushing all of my buttons. Between the club mess, the music Talon had blaring on the stereo, and the angry driver catching up to us, I felt nothing but rage. And anxiety. It bubbled deep inside of me, and I knew it would come out. Soon. And it was going to be fuckin' ugly.

CASH

I drove about twenty miles over the speed limit, but it did nothing to deter Rocky. He toyed with us, letting us get away before catching up and rear ending us again.

"Minx!" Talon cried out when he hit us again, only this time it was much harder.

The fucker just wanted to prove he could get to me—to us—any goddamn time he wanted. "Motherfucker!" I screamed at the top of my lungs when the next hit almost caused me to lose control of the van and we skidded toward the shoulder of the road. "Sorry, T."

"No worries," she said, white knuckling the grab handle as I gained control of the van.

We'd just crossed into the Brently city limits, and Rocky showed no signs of slowing down. I heard the telltale sound of a gang of motorcycles, and soon I saw the CAOS cuts in my mirror, gaining momentum behind Rocky. Rocky quickly cut down a side street, his tires squealing against the pavement. He obviously didn't expect CAOS to come to our rescue.

The bikes flanked us on all sides, taking us off the highway and escorting us all the way to Talon and Mick's house. "Safe and sound, *chica*."

"Thank you, Minx." She reached across the gear shift and hugged me tight. "Thanks."

"No problem." I sighed and tried to keep a smile on my face, but it felt like a grimace even to me. "I won't be getting your Jade Dragon, but I'm sure Mick or one of the prospects can pick it up for you."

Her violet eyes frowned in confusion. "You're not coming in?"

"Nah. I need some time alone. I'll call you soon. Promise."

"You sure?"

I nodded. "Yep." I wasn't okay, but Talon didn't the stress of my shit weighing on her pregnant body. "Spend the rest of the day with your feet up. Please."

She smiled. "Okay, Minx. Thanks again. Love you."

CASH

"Love you, too," I bit out as Mick pulled her from the car and wrapped her in his arms. I pulled away from the crowd and made my way home in a daze. I hadn't seen or recognized anything but somehow, I arrived safely at home. I climbed the steps and flipped all three locks behind me, keeping the lights off as I made my way to a nice hot bath.

I took a bath hoping a long, hot soak would calm me, but it wasn't working. Every time I closed my eyes, I saw memories that wouldn't quit. No matter how much time had passed, I could still hear the screeching tires of the van as it peeled out with me inside. The pounding club music of the 'parties' I was forced to work. The grunts and groans of those crotchety old bastards thrusting on top of me. The sounds of fists and open hands smacking skin. It was too fucking much and it was ruining my bath.

I climbed out and wrapped a big comfy robe around me. It was the kind you get from fancy hotels only I bought this one just for me. I padded to the living room and sat in the dark, firing up a joint in hopes that it would quiet the roaring noise in my head.

A furious pounding started at my front door, and I already knew it would be the green-eyed devil haunting my dreams. Another long pull until I felt the sweet satisfaction of oblivion and I stood, checking the peephole before pulling the door open and shoving down my body's response to his innate masculinity. His overwhelming presence and brooding sensuality. I gave him a quick once-over and returned to my seat on the sofa.

"Are you all right?" He was breathless and angry looking, but I couldn't bring myself to care. Not now.

I couldn't see him in the dark, but stared at his silhouette as I took another hit, the cherry tip was the only thing lighting up the room. "I'm great," I answered, sounding distinctly solemn, even to my own ears.

"Why didn't you wait for me to get to Talon's place?" Thick arms crossed over his broad chest, and

CASH

I could feel the weight of his stare even though I couldn't see it.

"Didn't know you were coming," I answered honestly, too. Not after all the years I'd been missing. Kidnapped. And no one ever came for me. And, I wasn't about to be waiting for help that would never come. Never again.

Finally, he moved and set his big body beside me as close as he could get. He wrapped his strong arms around me and buried his face in my hair. "I was so fucking worried, Minx."

"Sorry."

"God," he kissed my hair and held me tighter in relief. It was nice to have someone who gave a damn. "How are you, really?"

I didn't want to talk, but I also didn't want to be alone. If I didn't give him an answer, he'd probably leave, and I didn't want to be a bitch to Cash. He was the nicest man I knew, with the exception of Magnus who'd saved me. I answered him as honestly as I could. "I'm fine, Cash. I'm always fine."

"Well, I'm not," he said in a rough and gravelly voice thick with concern. Cash pulled my chin toward him until our eyes clashed in the darkness and claimed my mouth in a gut-wrenching kiss that stole my breath, my resolve, and my ability to think straight. He kissed me so long and hard I knew he was assuring himself that I was all right as he worked out his own demons on my mouth.

I was more than happy to let him work out his shit on me because I was determined to use his body to work out a few of my own problems. But I needed more than his hands and his mouth. I needed every inch of that big body to make me forget that once again my life wasn't my own. Pulling back from him, I stood and flicked on a light. If we were about to get naked, I needed at least some light to stare at the magnificence that was Cash's body. Then I untied my robe and let it fall to the floor.

CASH

"Minx," he groaned and pulled me back to him until I straddled his lap, resting right on his jean-covered erection. "You're so soft." He kissed my neck on both sides before sliding his tongue across my collarbone. "So fuckin' sweet."

His softly spoken words were too much. I covered his mouth with mine, deepening the kiss until he was so hungry for me he didn't need words. Big, strong hands kneaded my ass and pressed us closer together until his hard cock rubbed against me, and I gasped and whimpered. "Yes, Cash." My voice was just barely a whisper as he pulled a nipple in his mouth, first nipping it with his teeth and then sucking until my hips took on an urgent circular motion.

"I wanna fuck you so bad, baby," he groaned and moved to the other nipple.

It thrilled me that I could enjoy being with a man this way, letting him bring me pleasure. Cash always made sure I was satisfied. He never just thrust into me until he got his and left. Like now, he kissed his way down my body until I leaned back over his legs to give him full access. Then one thick finger slid into my pussy and I cried out, letting the first flutters of pleasure grip me and pull me under. It was fast and out of control, the orgasm jolted me out of my own head. "Cash," I whispered over and over.

"This time we're using the damn bed," he growled and stood, leaving me to wrap my legs around him though I knew he wouldn't let me fall. Unless he was tossing me on the bed, that is. I sat up on my elbows so I could watch him undress, watch the way the muscles in his chest and abs played against the dim lamp of my bedroom. The tattoos all over his body were like small works of art that I would love to explore, but now I was too wet and swollen for more of him.

"You really are gorgeous."

His gaze darkened as he kicked free of his pants and socks, and those gray boxer briefs that hugged strong thighs and cupped his cock so tempting that my mouth watered. "I'm just a man, Minx, you," he leaned over me and swiped his tongue through my pussy, making my hips buck up, "you are a fucking goddess."

I didn't believe him, but the way he dotted my body with soft kisses rendered me speechless. Never had a man touched me with so much tenderness. So gentle and caring. Not that Cash ever hurt me, but things were explosive, combustible between us. Fast and hard and furious. This was something else. When he finally reached my mouth, he devoured it in a slow, deeply sensual kiss that brought tears to my eyes. "God yes," I moaned when his cock slowly sank into my pussy until he was buried to the hilt. He stayed that way for too long as though he didn't need more, just to be there, inside me. "Please, baby."

My words set him moving, but again, this was no fast and hard coming together. Tonight, his strokes were slow and deep, almost drugged in the way he built me up. He kissed the same way, his tongue moved as slow and languid as the rest of him, but I was a slave to his unspoken commands. Forehead to forehead, we stared as he went deeper and deeper, our bodies slicked with sweat and each other as we climbed that mountain together. "Minx," he growled and hooked his arms under my legs, pumping faster but still so deep I thought we were becoming one.

"Cash, please. I need you." He switched positions again at my words, grabbing my ass with one hand and spearing his fingers in my hair with the other. His kiss took me up and his body drove so deep I knew I was powerless against the onslaught of sensations and emotions swamping me. Then I fell apart, shaking and shuddering and quivering my way through my orgasm while he pumped faster and faster until his own orgasm roared through him—and me—for long tense moments.

"Damn, Minx. You slay me."

"Ditto." I turned my head because I couldn't let him see the tears leaking from my eyes. I didn't understand it, but I knew those tears meant something. In my experience, there was only one reason a woman cried during or after sex, and what happened between us just now, wasn't it. That meant

CASH

it was something big and I didn't think I was strong enough to deal with yet.

If ever.

KB Winters

Chapter Six

Cash

Lying in bed like we were, with Minx resting her head on my bare chest, one leg and arm flung across my body, it almost felt like we were more than whatever the fuck we were. Something normal, like a couple I guess. The only sounds in the room was our heavy breathing as it returned to normal.

There was that fucking word again.

Normal.

I didn't know what it was or why it loomed so big between us, but I didn't want to think about it. I only wanted to think about the soft strip of skin my hand moved up and down in a slow, soothing motion. The fact that she didn't smack my hand away was a good sign. Then her soft voice broke through the quiet.

"I was thirteen-years-old. Hanging out at the park with my friend, Chloe, practicing our soccer skills for tryouts the next week. This lady came up to us and she looked normal, like she could have been one of my mom's church friends with her mom jeans and short flipped out hairdo, so I didn't think anything of it when she said her daughter was missing. Stupid me offered to help her look." Her voice shook and her hand trembled in circles on my stomach. "By the time I realized we were too far from the park it was too late. She'd already shoved me into the back of a windowless van. Sometimes, at night, I can still hear the sound of those tires peeling away from the curb. In a big-ass hurry even though no one was chasing us."

Her voice barely contained any emotions. It was rote, almost robotic but I didn't dare interrupt. Sharing this was a big step, and I refused to fuck it up.

"That night we stopped at a house somewhere, I don't know, but we hadn't been on the road more than a few hours because it had just gone dark when we got there. Maybe we were still in Indiana, but I didn't know. They put me in a room with ten other girls ranging in age from nine to sixteen. It was pitch black and there were no windows and just a few buckets in the room for us. As toilets."

I held her tighter but bit my tongue to mask the anger building in my gut on her behalf. She didn't need that right now. This was her shit, not mine.

"I got moved around the east coast for a while, New York. That's where they made sure I knew...who was boss. It took a couple months, a few busted ribs and a concussion to learn, but I did. Then I spent some time in Chicago. It was really bad there, but I couldn't let myself succumb to the drugs like the other girls. As long as I did what I was told, they didn't force them into me. Then there was Denver, Albuquerque, Vegas and Portland. When Magnus found me in the back of that truck I was headed to Mexico."

She fell silent for so long, and I felt like a jackass because I had no clue what to say to her. It explained so much about her quirks, but fuck, it also broke my heart for her. Made me angry enough to use my military skills to exact revenge for her. "I'm sorry you had to go through that, baby."

"Yeah, me, too," she sighed, and then rested her chin on the hand over my heart so she could look at me. "Do you know you're the only person I've ever had sex with that I wanted to? Ever?"

Damn, there was nothing else she could have said to get to me. Fuck. I felt honored that she'd given herself to me, but I didn't want her to stay in that dark place. Not for me. "It's because I'm so irresistible," I joked and tightened my grip on her, smacking a kiss on her forehead. "I can't say I'm not glad you chose me, but fuck, I want to kill the pieces of shit who did this to you."

She gave a wistful smile. "Good luck. That's all I dreamed about my first year out. But I don't know anyone's real names or addresses, so I gave up. I guess the shit today just brought it all to the surface." She blew out a long, shaky breath and pushed off me before sliding from the bed. "Now you know my story," she said, and moments later I heard her in the

CASH

kitchen. She stayed there for a few minutes and I let her, gave her the distance she needed after that.

"Thank you for telling me," I told her when she returned to bed with two glasses of water in her hands.

"Thanks for coming to check on me." She flashed a smile and placed her head on my chest again, this time right over my heart.

I opened my mouth to say something, hell to say anything. To tell her I would always check on her, but I didn't. I didn't know what she needed—wanted—to hear. By the time I found the words, her breathing was slow and deep. She'd fallen asleep. I gently tucked us under the blankets and held her tight through a restless, fitful sleep.

She cried out, kicked, and twitched in her sleep, and I realized why she never let me stay the night. And suddenly it all became so fucking clear I could have kicked myself for not realizing it sooner. Why she didn't have food delivered and why this little cottage had a tricked out surveillance system.

Yeah, it made sense, but what the fuck was I supposed to do with it?

***

"You haven't heard from her at all?"

I shook my head, pissed off and confused as hell about Minx's disappearance. In the passenger seat of Mick's old ass truck, I sulked as we headed to a town just over the border for our meeting with Lazarus. "Nope, she was quiet but fine the last time I saw her." Which was the morning after she revealed her past to me. We made love on and off throughout the night, and she made me breakfast before kicking me out with a kiss that I could still feel on my lips. "I blame myself," I told Mick. I was too fucking focused on whether or not I could handle what she had said that I didn't pay as much attention as I should have. She couldn't have been fine after reliving all that.

And I'd done fuck all to help her.

"Talon said she left a note."

CASH

"Yeah." It just said, "Thanks for everything. I need to clear my mind for a while. That was it. No promise to fucking return or check in. Nothing. Just peace out, see ya when I fucking see ya. Adios, motherfucker."

"*Can* you handle it? I think you better figure that out before she comes back."

If she comes back. "I can handle a lot. What I can't fucking handle is running."

Mick's sigh said he thought I was a dumb shit. "Her parents never found her, and as far as she knows never even looked for her. No one saved her until Magnus, and even he left."

Well shit. I hadn't thought of it like that. "Eyes up." I didn't have time to worry about it now that we closed in on our destination. I didn't fucking trust Lazarus as far as I could throw his little Mexican ass, and if he wanted to try some shit, we would be ready. Lazarus and four of his men leaned against a black SUV, smoking and laughing when we pulled up in front of the meeting spot. It was near a crowded market which made it difficult to watch our backs, but the objective here was simple. Keep an eye on Roddick and Lazarus.

We stepped from the truck, and the man's face lit up. "Gentlemen, to what do I owe this pleasure?"

Before we could say a word, Roddick rode up on his bike and dismounted, slowly ambling to where we stood with Lazarus just inches from us. "Lazarus. We got some news you might want to hear, *amigo*."

"I'm listening," he said in that deep heavily accented voice that was just a touch girly.

"Word on the street is that your new transport is selling your shit on the side."

"Not possible," Lazarus laughed and rolled his eyes. Lazarus stood tall and brushed his way too long hair from his eyes, but the lines around his eyes were tight.

"Tell that to the Black Bastards and Grim Reapers. Hell, you can even ask the Dragons." He named a few of the other clubs in the area, and I saw the lines around Lazarus' mouth tighten.

CASH

His eyes flared at the last name because they'd gone to war two years ago with the Dragons over the synthetic drugs the Chinese were selling. The war killed Lazarus' young brother, Julio. "The fuck you say?"

"You heard me," Roddick told him. "You did me a solid recently, so I'm returning the favor. That's all." He walked away and hopped on his bike.

"*Gracias*," he called out, laughing when Roddick only waved in return.

Mick and I jumped back in the truck and followed Rod, along with the other guys we had nearby, back to Brently. We didn't even have time to get comfortable before I spotted it. "Burning rubber, two o'clock," I said, and Mick went on alert as I knew he would. In the desert, the enemies always staged a distraction right before an attack.

Mick groaned and flashed his lights up ahead to signal the rest of them that trouble was brewing. "Fucking fuck!" He smacked the steering wheel when

Roddick fell off his bike a quarter mile up the road. "Shit!"

We caught up to them quickly, all the guys surrounding Roddick to protect him from the bullets flying across the highway. I jumped out and went around to the driver's side with my gun in hand, opening fire and shielding the guys so they could get Roddick to the truck without being hit. I heard an anguished grunt and knew one of them had been hit. I emptied my clip just to be sure then hopped in the back with Roddick while Mick raced back to the clubhouse.

The truck came to a screeching halt outside the clubhouse, and we carried Roddick inside. We had a medical room in the back and put him on the bed, cutting off his jeans and getting him some water. We all knew the fucking drill, but it didn't mean we weren't worried about our Prez. "Go get Cherie," I yelled. She was a nurse and Baz's older sister which meant she knew how to be discreet. We paid for discreet.

CASH

"She's on her way already," Baz said as he rushed in with towels, an IV drip, and Jack Daniels. "How you holdin' up, Prez?"

"Just fucking great, Baz," he said, smiling around a grimace. "Don't I look it?"

"Pretty as ever, bro. Just a tad bloody for my taste," he said as blood soaked through Roddick's shirt.

Roddick laughed and pulled the cap off the bottle of Jack. "Ah, thanks." He offered a smile and smacked his lips, chugging back a heavy swig. "Bullet went out, so I'll be good," he said after Jack started to work his legendary magic.

"All right, Roddick, what have you got for me?" Cherie rushed in all soft blonde curls and no nonsense attitude.

"You finally get a peek at these sexy legs," he joked, making her do the impossible. Smile.

"Easier ways to show off, you know?" She had her gloves on and bent low to examine the wound.

"We're going back for your bike, Rod. You're in good hands," Mick told him with an amused smile.

"Be careful," he told us, but his gaze stayed on me. "Get my bike and then go deal with your shit because you know what this means."

I knew what he was saying, and I nodded before I spoke the word we were all thinking but no one had said. "War."

CASH

Chapter Seven

Minx

I spent a week walking along the beach from early in the morning until late at night, and it hadn't been nearly enough. I rented a surfboard and just sat in the water letting the waves toss me around while I tried to sort my shit out. I needed more time because my head was nowhere near clear, and the nightmares were back. But I had a life to get back to, or more accurately, I had a house and a small business that I couldn't abandon if I wanted to keep food in my belly and gas in my car.

I rolled back into Brently in the early afternoon and kept my promise to stop at Talon's first thing. "Hey," I said when she pulled open the door with a wide-eyed smile.

"Minx! I'm so glad to see you." She yanked me inside and wrapped me as close as her belly would allow in a choking hug. "I was so worried about you."

"You don't need to worry. I'm always fine."

"That's what worries me," she said and poured two glasses of iced tea. "No one is always fine, girl, not even you. That means you're internalizing it."

"It's how I deal, T, but I'm trying." She opened her mouth to argue, but I held up the box I carried in to stop her. "Now we can talk about that, or we can talk about the wedding gifts I found while I was away."

She smiled, and when her gaze slid to the box for the third time, I shoved it across the table. She pulled out the vintage twenties style veil and gasped. "I love it!" When she spotted the light blue gothic style garter the waterworks began. "Thank you!"

"You're welcome" I said, chuckling a little. "How have you been?" The hairs on the back of my neck stood, and my spine went stock still the longer it took her to talk.

"Well, Cash has been worried sick about you." She gave me an admonishing look, but I willed my entire being to stay still.

CASH

"I figured he would be, but I just needed to get away." I wouldn't apologize for that, not even to Talon. I listened with a sickness I couldn't name in my stomach as she told me about Roddick. "Is he okay?"

She shrugged. "Mick says he will be, but tensions are high in town, and they're talking war."

"Looks like my timing is spot on, as usual. Great." I stood and hugged Talon, letting her squeeze me tight because I knew she worried about me. "I probably have a lot of stuff waiting for me at home, so I'd better get going. Gotta make that money."

"Come back tomorrow for dinner," she ordered in that tone that told me that arguing would be pointless, so I waved and started the engine. I stopped at the store and picked up a few things before stopping at the club.

"Hey, Roddick, how are you?" He looked like shit, pale with red-rimmed eyes.

"I've been better, kid. What are you doing here?"

"Talon told me you were hurt, so I came to bring you a few things." I unloaded the box of his favorite snacks and the tablet he kept hidden behind the bar. "Might make recovery less boring."

He laughed and looked at everything. "Thanks, Minx." He tore open a box of Suzy-Q's and bit into one of the chocolatey cakes with a loud moan. "I'm sure Talon told you what's been going on, so you know why I'm going to have the prospects man the bar this week?"

It was clear I was no longer needed, and that was just fine with me. These guys had become like a weird, horny family to me, but they weren't the first family I lost. If I was smart—and I liked to think I was—they'd be my last. "Fine. I need to go so, feel better."

"Minx wait—"

"It's fine, I get it. Take care of yourself," I told him and rushed from the room, through the club and back to my car. I knew what had to be done now, and it made me glad I'd picked up a few bags of groceries

CASH

for myself. I spent the next few days holed up at the cottage, sewing and studying, studying and sewing. In between I would eat and sleep while music played constantly. I was always busy and it was always loud, just how I wanted it.

By day three my mind began to wander to Cash, wondering if he was okay or how pissed off he was. But I knew the truth was he'd already given up on me like everyone else had, only this time I couldn't blame him. I pushed and pushed and in the end, he realized what I'd always known—I just wasn't worth the effort.

Keeping weird hours and an impossible workload had taken its toll, and I fell asleep in the middle of the fourth day of confinement. I woke up to someone pounding on the door with the strength of ten men and instantly I went on alert, running to check the surveillance before pulling the door open. "Yes?"

He looked at me, green eyes furious yet relieved, and pushed his way inside, slamming and locking the door behind him. I wasn't worried because I knew he wouldn't hurt me, but still I took a step back. "Don't run away from me."

"I didn't run—"

He cut me off. "You did. You fucking did." He toed off his boots and pulled me into the living room where he wrapped me in his arms. "You told me about your past, freaked out, and ran."

Okay, now he was pissing me off. "So what if I did, Cash? I'm not your responsibility just because we had sex a few times."

"I refuse to even respond to that bullshit, Minx. Lie to yourself, sweetheart, but don't ever fucking lie to me." His voice was low and daunting as he brushed a whisper-soft kiss against my lips, so achingly tender I felt my eyes begin to sting.

"What are you doing here?"

"As soon as I found out you were back in town I came to check on you. Though it would have been nice to get a call or a text. Maybe a smoke signal." He leaned in and kissed me again and this time it was all hungry and frantic, demanding and desperate. I

CASH

couldn't resist his kisses if I wanted to, and I didn't want to. I missed him, and I told him so with my mouth. My tongue. "I'm glad you're okay, Minx, but goddammit I want to paddle your ass for making me worry so long."

I rolled my eyes up at him and smiled. "Promises, promises."

He tossed me over his shoulder and carried me to the bedroom where he tossed me on the bed and kept his promise. "I told you, Minx, I'm a man of my word.

I was starting to see that.

KB Winters

***

Willingly sharing my body with someone was an act of trust and intimacy that scared the hell out of me. I just wish I'd realized it before now—before another earth-shattering night spent with Cash's big body wrapped around mine. The man was a master lover, using his entire body to bring mine to unspeakable heights. And he made the most delicious noises when I explored his big, strong body. I woke up and turned to him, and only one word came to mind. *More*. I wanted—no I needed—more of this man. My body buzzed with need like I just couldn't get enough of him, and that scared the shit out of me.

Yesterday morning after he kissed me until I was on the verge of begging him to stay, I gave him my number. A way to get in touch with me when he was worried or wanted to come by. Now that he knew why it was a big deal, I knew he'd call even if it was to tell me he was on my doorstep waiting.

I smiled as I thought about how grumpy he got when he was worried because an alpha like him didn't do vulnerability. It was nice to have someone in my life who seemed to give a damn about me, but it would take some time to get used to. Probably a long time.

Or maybe I was fooling myself, thinking I could have anything that resembled normal after what I'd been through. A guy like Cash would probably want someone with less baggage, less damage. Eventually the nightmares, my hang ups about security and visitors, all of it would grow tiresome. He'd get sick of it just when I was getting used to having him around, and then he would leave. I sighed. Why did the thought of losing him make my heart feel hollow with a dull ache? I didn't like that shit. Not at all.

I couldn't get used to this, I had to back away.

No more sleepovers.

No more sex.

No more Cash.

Fuck. Fuck, fuck, fuck! "No. More. Cash!" I said out loud just to get it through my thick skull.

Yet when he called later that afternoon, I answered halfway through the second ring. Weak, that's what I was. Fucking weak. "Yeah?"

"What do you want for dinner?"

"I'm already cooking so if you want, you can stop by." He went silent because apparently, I surprised him as much as I'd surprised myself.

"I'll be there in ten. Wear something sexy," he chuckled and disconnected the call.

"Fucking weak, that's what you are." I told myself that at least three times before I put the chicken, potatoes, and vegetables in the oven to roast. And though I wouldn't change my clothes—a girl had to have some pride, after all—the cook time would allow for one more taste of that sweet man.

Fifteen minutes later a knock sounded and I went to the door, ready to give him crap for being late. I paused a fraction of a second before turning the knob as a weird sensation skittered down my spine. But it was too late. I groaned. "What are you doing here,

CASH

Wagman? And how the fuck do you even know where I live?

"Why, sweetheart, Minxy baby, I came for you," he said with that smarmy smile that made my stomach turn. "Ain't you happy to see me?"

I didn't get the chance to answer because a meaty fist flew at my face too fast to move, and then shit went black.

KB Winters

Chapter Eight

Cash

Minx's invitation surprised the hell out of me, but I wasn't one to ask why she had a change of heart. I grabbed a bottle of tequila and her favorite pistachio ice cream and made my way to the small cottage. I climbed the stairs with a smile already splitting my face, ready to kiss the hell out of her, but that all quickly faded away as I caught the door partially open. And was that…blood on the floor?

I pushed it open and called out for her. "Minx, you in here?" I already knew the answer, but I went in and checked all the rooms to make sure she wasn't hurt in there somewhere. She wasn't. I pulled out my phone knowing I would need the help of CAOS to get her back. "Mick, get to Minx's ASAP. Her door was open, and there's blood on the floor." I hung up without waiting for a reply.

I went back to the guest bedroom and pulled open the sliding doors that held the surveillance system of the property, going through the footage since I last spoke to her. Already a sick feeling settled in my gut. Wagman knocked and she answered the door far too quickly to have checked first, so I knew she thought it was me, and that was confirmed at the confused expression on her face at her visitor. They spoke briefly and then that motherfucker punched her, right in the face. He caught her before she hit the ground, making sure he felt up her titties as he did.

"What's up?"

I looked up at Mick feeling more helpless than I had since leaving the Navy. "Wagman. That sorry motherfucker has Minx." I raked my hands through my hair and paced the room while Mick viewed the video. *Hang on, baby, I'm coming,* I promised her.

"Let's ride, Cash!" Mick ordered, breaking my frantic state, and I followed him out, making sure to close and lock her door. Full of rage and unable to concentrate, I didn't even know what the fuck to do

CASH

first. Where would he have taken her? That's what I needed to know so I could save Minx and then fucking annihilate Wagman.

Mick put a hand to my chest to stop my pacing on the street. "Dante called. He saw Wagman in a truck headed inside a building near the docks. Owned by Lazarus," he added ominously.

I nodded. "Weapons. I only have my nine and a blade, you?"

Mick grinned. "I got Big Mama"—he smacked his hip affectionately where his .45 was— "a .38, plus a blade."

I nodded with a wry grin. "That's all?" He shrugged and stole the keys from my hand before hopping into the passenger seat. "Let's stop at my place first."

"She'll be fine, Cash. Wagman just wants to fuck with you for putting his shit on blast to Lazarus."

I didn't believe him, but I nodded because all we could do now was plan and hope like hell that she was okay. When we got to the house, we packed enough firepower to fuck up a small army and then we got back on the road. "Let's go get the girl and fuck some shit up."

Mick nodded as he slid his phone in his pocket. "Just talked to Roddick, and Lazarus' men will meet us at the gate. We'll pick up a few guys on our way to the docks."

I stepped on the gas not needing to be told twice.

Hang on, baby.

***

Minx

When I came to, I had no idea where the fuck I was. It was dark, quiet and smelled like the ocean. The last thing I remembered was Wagman throwing a mean jab straight to my face, which explained the throbbing in my right cheek and the swelling in my eye. I began to panic because this was all too familiar. *No, not again.* I couldn't go through that again. I would die fighting, but I hoped and prayed Cash would prove to be my hero and swoop in and save me, even though I knew he didn't have the slightest clue of where I was. For now, I was on my own.

My wrists and ankles were shackled, a long straight metal pole keeping them separated. The kind of contraption I remembered all too fucking well.

Breathe. I needed to focus on my breathing. I didn't know where I was or who was nearby, and I didn't need to alert anyone that I was awake. I heard a distinct thump-drag, thump-drag, and I closed my eyes to get a better listen. *Thump-drag, thump-drag.* It was the walk of an injured person.

The lights flickered on and I blinked a few times to get my eyes to adjust, and I saw him. Rocky. I also saw my surroundings, an empty warehouse with a few boxes stacked against the wall. Probably drugs. "Good, you're awake. I would have hated for you to sleep through our first fuck." He stroked his cock slowly, licking his lips as his beady little gaze raked over my body.

I stayed silent because I'd learned its power by the time I was fifteen. The men who wanted to hurt me got off on hearing me scream, seeing that fear in my eyes. Take that away from them and I gained the upper hand.

"Nothing to say, Minxy? You spread it for old Magnus, spread it for CJ. Now you're gonna spread it all for me."

Bile rose in my throat at the sight of him, greasy and sweating, obviously an infection from that disgusting wound on his shoulder. Still, I kept my expression neutral, my gaze blank.

Rocky did the *thump-drag, thump-drag* thing again to move closer, this time so he could touch me. "First, I'm gonna fuck that pretty little mouth, deep down your throat, sweetheart, until you fucking choke on my cock. Let's just say"—his finger gently brushed up the inside of my thigh— "that I'm gonna wreck all of you. That Boy Scout CJ probably won't even want you when I'm done. *If* there's anything left."

CASH

Fear. I should've felt fear but I didn't. I didn't feel anything. Numb and cold. My body was shutting down. Again. It was how I'd survived all those years, but this time wasn't like that. This time I would fight. I would either be free or dead when this was done. I was prepared for either.

"Still got nothing to say, bitch? Don't worry, I'll have you screaming real soon." He leaned in, and I almost puked at the combination of his infected wound and body odor. He grabbed my tits and squeezed hard, but I stayed quiet. "Fuck yeah. You got a great set of tits, bitch. You ever been titty fucked? I bet you have." He sneered but I kept my gaze on him, prepared for any sudden moves.

I gave him my best bored out of my mind look. "Nothing worse than being fondled by a decaying corpse I suppose."

He grinned before a greasy hand slammed down on my left cheek. "Fucking whore!"

My face throbbed, but I stayed silent. Not a gasp or a scream. I just absorbed the hit and stared at him like the little bitch he was.

"A tough girl, eh?" His fist landed hard in my stomach, knocking the breath out of me, but still, I said nothing. Another fist landed in the same spot, and the next three hit my ribs until I was pretty sure one of them cracked. "We'll see how tough you are before the day is over." His gaze was filled with hatred, rage. Then he balled up his fist and slammed it against my face two more times.

I was silent. Defiantly so.

"Don't think you're gonna be a quiet little mouse, because I'll make sure you ain't." He backhanded me and squeezed my tits again. His anger rose at my silence, and I saw the moment something changed in his eyes—they went dark and deadly intense. My shackles were released, the bar tossed aside, and he pushed me down on the moldy sofa with a leering smile. He climbed between my legs, rubbing his denim-clad cock against me. He tried to kiss me, but I turned my head which earned me another smack.

I held my breath as he rubbed against me while he removed my wrist shackles, moving my hips against him to keep him distracted.

"Oh yeah, you dirty little slut. You fucking like it," he grunted and pressed harder against me, licking my ear.

I let out the breath I was holding, and the scent of sickness swamped me. This was the perfect opportunity I realized, the scent so strong my eyes began to water. My hips moved faster against his, keeping him lost in lust while I found the source of the stench and dug my thumb good and deep into his shoulder, fighting back a gag as puss and blood oozed from the wound.

"You fucking bitch! I will fucking kill you!" He shouted and leaned back so he loomed over me, his fists coming down on my chest and face and stomach again. I was powerless to stop from this position so I covered my head as best I could, clenching my jaw through the blows. "I was just gonna fuck you good and hard but now, now I'm gonna make you hurt. Bleed." He backhanded me and stood back, picking up one of the straight bar shackles.

I braced myself for another hit—or worse. It wouldn't be the first time or the worst that's ever happened to me. Rocky was right about that. Only nothing happened. Nothing. Except his cry of pain followed by a scuffle and then the sound of more fists pounding flesh. I couldn't open my eyes, I was too shaken and too damn scared to see what was about to happen to me.

"Where is she, you piece of shit?" The voice was angry, no—full of rage. And it was a familiar voice.

"Cash?" Maybe I was hallucinating because there was no way he was actually here. For me. A hand wrapped around my arms and pulled them from my face. I stared up into dark brown eyes surrounded by smooth, youthful brown skin.

"Estás bien?"

CASH

I nodded. "*Si.*" I proved myself a liar as I tried to sit up and cried out in pain.

"Minx!" Cash was at my side moments later, lifting me gently while Mick held Rocky pinned against the wall by the throat. At least a dozen Hispanic men mixed in with CAOS members. "Did that fucker touch you?"

"Mostly with his fists." I tried for a smile, but Cash's worried face told me I failed, plus the cough that shook my body and pulled a cry from me.

"Let's go!" I looked up and noticed a familiar head of red hair had barked that order. Mick. Everyone began moving to do as their leader had said.

"Wait." The man who'd checked on me spoke, his voice deep and heavily accented. His men aimed their guns toward CAOS.

"What the fuck, man?" Mick frowned, his own gun aimed right at the shorter man whose vest named him a Mexican Devil.

"You go and take the girl. Lazarus wants to deal with this one himself. He says to tell you 'the problem will be solved'."

Cash and Mick communicated silently and having reached some agreement, they made their way to the door with me hanging on to Cash for dear life. The rest of the CAOS rescue team walked behind us, completely on alert for more trouble. "Good fucking riddance," Cash muttered and shook his head as his hands gently caressed my back.

Rocky cursed, "You fucking bitch, I'll kill you and your pretty little boyfriend. Fuck you all, pussies!" His venom faded as we moved closer to the waiting vehicles being guarded by the new prospects.

"You okay, Minx?" Mick's hand fell on my shoulder, his green eyes taking in what I was sure were bruises, busted lips, and judging by my vision, at least one eye was swollen shut.

I tried for a smile. "I've been better, Mick." I coughed and cried again, squeezing my eyes shut. "I think I need a hospital."

CASH

Chapter Nine

Cash

Holy fuck, I'd never been so fucking scared in my life. Not even when Mick, me, and our crew were pinned down by insurgents and our comm was down was I as afraid as I was entering that fucking warehouse. Hoping and even sending a prayer up to a God I'd given up on years ago that Minx would be all right.

As we drew closer, I heard the shit Rocky said to her. It wasn't pretty; some of it was just plain fucking disturbing, and I was pretty sure she'd be dealing with those scars longer than the physical ones. She'd likely suffer flashbacks if not full-blown PTSD in the coming weeks and months. But she impressed the hell out of me, using silence as a weapon against that weak asshole.

But seeing her bloody and bruised like that, hearing those blows rain down on her knowing I was

CASH

in no position to do shit about it killed me. I wanted to take care of Rocky myself, squeeze the life out of that sorry motherfucker so he knew who did it to him. But the club had to approve it.

All I gave a shit about now was Minx. She'd be okay in that her body would heal, but I worried about the rest of her. The part on the inside. The moment I saw Cherie I jumped to my feet. "How is she?"

Cherie's smile was grim. "She's okay. Got a busted rib and a few deep bruises, possibly a concussion. She said to tell you she's fine and you don't need to worry about her."

That I didn't need to...what the fuck? "What? No. Where is she?" I walked down the hall where Cherie pointed, stopping at the room number she'd called out to me. I steeled myself and took a deep breath outside her room before pushing in. "You don't think you're getting rid of me that easy, do you? I'm not letting you run away. Not again, baby girl."

She blinked once. Twice. Then one tear fell from her right eye, bruised and swollen shut. She looked away from me then tried to use her hair to hide the bruises on her face. "I need time, Cash."

"I got lots of time. I'm here and ready to listen."

She glared at me and I glared back until her gaze softened, her body relaxed. "I don't know if I can."

"Then talk to Talon, she's waddling around the waiting room ready to punch someone to get back here."

"Yet you're here," she challenged, tilting her head toward me.

I smiled and ran a hand over her hair. "I'm bigger than she is, and I think we've already established—I'm irresistible." She tried to laugh but gasped in pain. I put my hand to her rib. "Sorry, babe. Breathe." I inhaled and exhaled deeply so she would do the same.

"Thank you, Cash. For coming for me. For saving me." She wiped more tears as they fell. "I'm sorry I didn't expect you to. I should have."

CASH

I dropped down on the bed so we were eye to eye. "Always, babe." I wrapped her hands in mine and pressed a kiss to the bruises on her wrists. "Get some rest, sweetheart, I'll be right here. I promise."

"No." She shook her head. "I can't." I saw the fear in her eyes, and it just about tore me apart.

"I already know about the nightmares, Minx. Last time I stayed over you twitched and cried all night long." Her eyes burned with embarrassment, and she looked away. "Don't hide, Minx." I grabbed her chin so she had to look at me and brushed a kiss to her forehead. "Don't be embarrassed."

"I'm not."

I smiled and held her cheek, rubbing my thumb along smooth skin peppered with ugly purple bruises. "Whatever you say, babe. Now, sleep."

"You're bossy," she yawned.

"All part of the irresistible package that is me." I winked, and she giggled just as I hoped.

"You are pretty irresistible," she admitted, and I knew the meds were getting to her. "Thank you for rescuing me, Cash."

She drifted off on my shoulder, and I wrapped my arms around her as she fell asleep. Sleep didn't come quite so easily for me as I thought about her admission. It was the first time she'd complimented me outside of sex, and I knew it was too soon to hope, but I knew she was mine.

Mine.

It was the last word I thought before sleep claimed me, too.

***

Minx

"I know you're not ready to hear this yet, but I love you, Minx. You're prickly as hell and you love nothing more than giving me a hard time, but it only makes me want you more. I know you need to be strong because you've been through six kinds of hell, and I want you to be strong. Hell, I can help you be

CASH

stronger if you want, but dammit I don't want you weak. I love you strong, and I love that you trust me enough to be vulnerable. I promise never to betray that. I love you so much. Please don't use this as an excuse to run from me."

I still couldn't believe he'd said all that to me. I didn't know what to say or do in reply. That's not entirely true because as soon as he said that scary 'L' word I knew that was the strange feeling twisting my gut and squeezing my heart. *Love.* It was uncomfortable, made it hard to breath, stole all the moisture from my mouth, and made me want to be around him all the time. It had to be love.

Which meant I was totally screwed.

And a coward because I pretended to be asleep while he poured his heart out to me, and when he returned I kept the pretense up because I couldn't figure out how to respond. I knew how I felt, but it all was happening too soon. How could I trust that this was real? That it wasn't just wild and crazy sex combined with an intense situation?

I couldn't.

But I also couldn't have anticipated that a member of a biker gang would save me and help me start my new life. I never could've dreamed that I'd be making and selling dresses or that I would have a good man in my life who loved me. I had to be brave. I had to be the strong woman Cash saw when he looked at me. I started with a caress, stretching my arm to where his head lay on my lap, and ran my fingers through his hair.

He looked up and flashed that dimpled smile that never failed to turn me on and turn my insides to goo. "You're awake."

"So are you. I can't believe you slept here."

"Of course I did, I needed to make sure you were okay."

"In a building full of doctors and medicine?" The man took the overprotective alpha thing to the extreme.

CASH

"I needed to know for myself. Shit, Minx, hearing that asshole hit you and knowing I wouldn't get close enough in time, fuck, I wanted to kill that bastard."

I caressed his face. "I know, but you came for me. You came." I didn't know how to make him understand how much that act alone meant to me. "For years I wished my parents' or the police would come and save me, but no one ever did. It didn't even occur to me that you would come. When I heard your voice, I thought I was hallucinating."

He moved up to sit beside me and put his forehead to mine. "You're killing me, babe."

"I'm trying to say thank you, dork. For coming for me, for staying with me."

"Don't thank me. I needed to be here as much as you needed me, even if you didn't say so."

I returned his smile. "But I didn't say you shouldn't which is kind of the same thing."

He laughed and shook his head. "Minx, what am I going to do with you?"

I took a breath and looked at him, my big blond Boy Scout. His green eyes stared at me so full of some unknown emotion that stirred an emotion I was slowly coming to terms with. "Love me?"

"I already do."

Damn, he was good. "Oh damn, I love you too, Cash."

He chuckled at my groaned words. "Don't sound so excited about it, babe."

"I don't know shit about love or relationships. You know I'll screw it up."

"Not if I don't let you." He pressed a soft kiss to my mouth and muttered a curse over my split lip. "We'll talk and share and shit. I'm told that's how these things work."

I felt like he'd lifted a huge weight I didn't even know I'd been carrying. "If you're sure."

"I'm sure enough for the both of us. I know you'll catch up." He winked and gave his best panty-dropping smile.

CASH

"Because you're so irresistible?"

He kissed my forehead and nodded. "Now you're finally getting' it. I knew you were more than a smart mouth and a hot bod."

I couldn't help the laughter that bubbled out of me, or the screaming pain that tore through my ribs. "Ow, don't make me laugh." I cupped his face, unable to believe this man was mine. Loved me and wanted me to love him, too. "I do love you, but I'm terrified."

"Me, too. But we'll have each other, so we'll be all good," he said simply.

"Promise?"

"I promise."

"Then I'm in." And I was. Cash had given me something I didn't think I would ever have again. Love. I would cherish it and nourish it every damn day.

KB Winters

CASH

Epilogue

Minx *– 3 months later*

I wish I could say I didn't cry when my best friend said her vows that bonded her to the love of her life, but I bawled like a big ol' baby, which actually wasn't all that unusual for me these days. Talon looked so beautiful in her ice blue wedding gown, her skin glowed from all the love and the baby hormones.

Their ceremony was beautiful and quick, just how the bride wanted it, and she'd only tolerated about thirty minutes of photos, which I also appreciated. "You could leave the dress on if you wanted," I told her as I unzipped her.

"No way, I can't wait to put on that beautiful dress you made." She cast a glance at the blue maternity party dress I'd made as a surprise wedding gift when I was released from the hospital and cleared for movement. It took almost two months before all the bruises vanished and my ribs had healed. Sometimes

I swear I could still feel it broken in there, but Cash and my therapist both said it's all in my head. "How are you, girl, for real?"

I smiled at her in the mirror. "Getting better every day." It was true, I was. At least once I left the cottage I started to feel a little better each day. I didn't feel safe there, and Cash was more than happy to have me move in with him. "Do you think living with Cash is the right thing?"

Talon nodded. "Hell yeah! He loves you and you love him, but I'm guessing he knows how to help when you refuse to ask?"

"I needed to hear it. Sometimes I'm not sure if I'm scared because it's new for me or because it's just scary." I hugged her and then helped her into her dress and let her hair down. "Ready to celebrate?"

"Damn straight, babe!" She gave a little booty shake, and we went out into her backyard so the reception could officially begin, though everyone already had drinks in their hands.

CASH

I spotted Cash just as the first dance came to an end, and he came over to me. "Dance with me." He pulled me onto the dance floor and then into his arms where I was happy to be.

I looked up at him, stars in my eyes. "I'm so happy I took a chance on a Boy Scout."

He laughed and pulled me closer. "I think you mean an irresistible Boy Scout." He dipped me and gave me a whisper-soft kiss, peeking over my shoulder at the newlyweds. "That will be us someday."

I hoped with all my heart that was true. "Family, too?" I'd realized over the past few months just how badly I wanted that. Family.

He nodded and stole my breath with the intensity of his gaze. "Definitely."

"You mean it?" I felt hope build and swell in my chest as I imagined us having a backyard barbecue with a few little kids running around us.

"Fuck yeah. We'll start tonight."

I was glad to hear that because I had news to share with him tonight. In bed. "I love you."

He grinned. "Good thing I love you too, then," he joked the way he always did when I said it to him. Then his expression turned serious and worry built up in my belly. "I found your family. It's up to you what you do with the information, but I have it for you."

"W-w-what?"

"You heard me."

I couldn't believe it. He'd given me love when I didn't think I'd ever have it, and now he'd found my family. *If* I wanted them. "What did I do to deserve a guy like you?"

"Don't you know, Minx? You stole my heart."

"And I'm keeping it. Forever."

"Then you'll have to marry me."

I couldn't believe my ears. He'd been telling me for months he wanted to marry me, make me his wife, and I hadn't been able to believe it. Now though, I was ready. I nodded as tears filled my eyes. "Then we should probably get married before the baby is born."

Big green eyes widened in shock and then filled with happiness. "Baby? You're having my baby?" I nodded and a wide grin swept across my face.

"You know if we hurry, we might be able to catch the minister."

"Fuck yeah, baby. I'm there."

~The End.~

KB Winters

Acknowledgements

Thank you! I love you all and thank you for making my books a success!! I appreciate each and every one of you.

Thanks to all of my beta readers, street teamers, ARC readers and Facebook fans. Y'all are THE BEST!

And a huge very special thanks to my wonderful PA, Silla. Without you, I'd be a hot mess! With you, I'm a hot mess, but without your keen sense of organization and skills, I'd be a burny fiery inferno of hot mess!! Thank you!

And a very special thanks to my editor, Silla Webb (who sometimes has to work all through the night! See HOT MESS above!) Thank you for making my words make sense.

Copyright © 2017 BookBoyfriends Publishing LLC KB WINTERS

About The Author

KB Winters has an addiction to caffeine, tattoos and hard-bodied alpha males. The men in her books are very sexy, protective and sometimes bossy, her ladies are...well...bossier!

Living in sunny Southern California, the embarrassingly hopeless romantic writes every chance she gets!

You can connect with KB on Facebook (https://www.facebook.com/kbwintersauthor) and Twitter (http://twitter.com/kbwintersauthor)!

Printed in Great Britain
by Amazon